Sparkles

Sparkles

CHARMIN KARDON

ARCHWAY
PUBLISHING

Archway Publishing books may be ordered through booksellers or by contacting:

Archway Publishing
1663 Liberty Drive
Bloomington, IN 47403
www.archwaypublishing.com
1-(888)-242-5904

ISBN: 978-1-4808-1088-4 (sc)
ISBN: 978-1-4808-1089-1 (e)

Library of Congress Control Number: 2014915457

Printed in the United States of America.

Archway Publishing rev. date: 9/17/2014

I would like to take this opportunity to thank my family and friends for their continued love and support.

"Authors, should follow the rules but live outside the box"

Forever Love

Two young people met by chance, unaware that their relationship would evolve into a lusty love affair and then marriage years later.

Charmin Kardon was very confined and old-fashioned, whereas Maxwell Long was open to new ideas and needed freshness and creativity.

From the moment Maxwell saw Charmin, he craved the warmth of her body. His eyes scanned her curves and full, large breasts, creating a sense of ownership. Charmin's temperate mannerisms and soft-spoken voice gave way to a sexual being Maxwell was sure he would soon possess.

Maxwell had a lusty appetite for sex. Charmin had to learn how to share his desires and needs without passing judgment, while also understanding how to manage her own desires so as not to become possessive. In return, Maxwell searched for a balance that allowed him to be free, yet married as well.

Sometimes one has to bend the rules a little to find "happily ever after," a quest that varies for everyone.

This manuscript is a depiction of my youth in many ways. Although much of the content is fictitious, there are semblances that hold true to my experiences.

The male character, Maxwell Long, is a strong, educated go-getter who finds love early in his youth but struggles with his ego, pride, and commitment issues. The idea of sex is what motivates him and is the driving force he needs to succeed in life. Within his unguarded self lies a tender heart in need of love and affection, but no one is supposed to see or know that side of him except the one he pines for: Charmin.

The female character, Charmin Kardon, is an independent thinker and an educated go-getter who also finds love in her youth, but she struggles with insecurities and rejection. Unlike her partner, Charmin's quest is driven by loyalty, devotion, and the desire to satisfy her man. Her quiet side hides a rage of jealousy, which is sheltered even from the love of her life.

The setting is embedded in familiar events that occurred throughout the couple's reunion. There is an energy binding them together that words cannot explain. As if by design, it appears they were destined to be together even from their first encounter. The long courtship that followed is evidence of this. Maxwell takes comfort in Charmin's body, which gives him the sexual fulfillment of control and domination. A man likes to feel revered and thought of as all knowing because it feeds his ego.

As much as they enjoy each other's company, there is still much unsaid between them. Maxwell lives in a world of seclusion, only surfacing for food and sex before retreating to his isolation. Contrary to her partner, Charmin finds herself walking on eggshells at times, so as not to create imbalance in their relationship or anger Maxwell and create a wall between them. Although she is a good judge of character, it is difficult for her to read Maxwell because he is so guarded. Charmin is seen as pokerfaced. One can seldom see past her façade—which is just the way she likes it.

If Maxwell had his way, they would live in a bed, naked, having sex all the time, whereas Charmin would prefer to be at a club, dancing the night away. Charmin has never been one to pay a lot of attention to details. Her philosophy is to go with the flow and work things out as they materialize.

Although men do not have "cycles," they certainly share the mood swings. For two people to love each other unconditionally, irrevocably, and unequivocally means to understand the other's differences, their irritating quirks, and the thread that holds the love together.

No one really knows his or her destiny. Many folks take a lifetime to find a soul mate, while others are fortunate enough to find love early in life. Either way, there are no handbooks; therefore, mistakes are made across the board. Only those who move forward and grab the bull by the horns understand their journey.

Chapter 1

Holding hands, they rushed through the lobby of the Omni Hotel and to their room. His adrenaline was pumping because the San Francisco 49ers had defeated the Cincinnati Bengals 20–16 in Super Bowl XXIII.

Just as the elevator doors opened, he yanked her inside, pinning her against the elevator wall. His wide eyes focused only on her as he squeezed her breasts. His lips tightened against hers as he forced his tongue into her mouth to dance with hers while his hands moved vigorously over her face and body.

In the midst of their passion, a chiming sound filled the air, alerting them the elevator was approaching a floor. They paused, looking at each other, unaware if either had selected level eight. The final chime notified them the doors were opening. They composed themselves quickly, and both held naughty smiles as other guests entered the elevator.

Once the elevator reached their floor, Maxwell and Charmin stepped out quickly.

"I can't wait to be with you, baby," Maxwell whispered.

"I know. I have never felt this way about anyone. You are very special to me."

"Me too. I love you, Charmin," he said as they hastily walked toward the room.

"Love you too, Maxwell," Charmin smiled.

In the bathroom, Charmin looked at her reflection and thought to herself, *Are you ready, Charmin?* Her actions answered the question by undressing. Knowing Maxwell would be inside her for the first time, her thoughts began to wander again, thinking about what actions she needed to take. She wanted their first experience to be special and memorable. At that thought, she refreshed her makeup and brushed her hair. She nervously walked out of the bathroom, and there Maxwell stood. She could tell he was admiring her lacy purple bra and matching panties. It was then Charmin remembered purple was his favorite color.

Maxwell stood tall and anxious but was still dressed in his gray Jordan T-shirt and blue jeans. They walked toward each other as he reached out to embrace her. She locked her arms around his waist, still trying to calm herself down and breathe. She felt his lips hot against her forehead and then against her lips. The wetness of his mouth allowed her to trace his lips with her tongue as they kissed.

She could feel him unfasten the hooks of her bra as he moved his hands to caress the small of her back. Maxwell grabbed her ass, tracing his fingers along its roundness. She wondered if he could hear or feel her heart racing with anticipation. She felt the heat and wetness between her thighs. Maxwell's mouth and tongue kissed and licked her neck and shoulder before reaching their intended target: her breasts. He bit and sucked on her nipples with a forceful grip, causing soft moans to escape her lips.

Charmin wanted to feel Maxwell's hot flesh against her smooth skin, so she reached over and helped pull off his T-shirt, exposing his toned physique. He continued as if uninterrupted, sucking and biting her nipples while his hands wandered all over her voluptuous body. His face lowered, now pressed against the center of her thighs. She could hear him breathing as he inhaled the scent of her pheromones and licked against her panties.

Maxwell smiled, looked up at Charmin, and said, "I want to see what you look like. Can I pull down your panties?"

Overcome with sexual thoughts, Charmin's mouth opened, only to respond with a rushed yes.

Maxwell proceeded to do as he'd asked, allowing the garment to rest against her ankles. He examined her closely with his fingers and his mouth. As he did this, Charmin felt lightheaded and reached out for the dresser so not to lose her balance. Maxwell parted her lips with his tongue, sending a heightened sensation coursing throughout her body—something she had never felt before. He continued licking and sucking on her minora while his fingers parted and entered her.

The illumination of the room changed. She no longer remembered where she was, only that he was with her. She got on her knees and unzipped his pants to free his manhood, and then she opened her mouth over his shaft. She sucked and licked him up and down while her hands firmly cupped his balls. His voice repeated, "Oh yeah."

She continued to suck and milk the pre-love juice out of his shaft. She felt his hands reach under her, pulling her onto him. Maxwell lifted her against his chest before laying her on the bed. The thickness of his shaft against her tight, wet canal created a strong pressure that pulled her apart as her body took him in. Hard thrusts resulted in moaning and heavy breathing, and she dug her nails into his back with every motion.

She opened her eyes and noticed her legs elevated in the air slightly over her head; she was still wearing her high heels. His kisses were hard and wet, but loving and compassionate.

Maxwell loved Charmin, and she loved him.

How They Met

It was a warm, beautiful day filled with possibilities and adventure as Charmin's family ventured out of New York City en route to St.

Petersburg, Florida, a family trip to cap off the summer before school started. Just beginning her senior year, Charmin had a voluptuous figure. Her family was European, which gave her an exotic flair. Her eyes were deep brown, and her hair was brown with a hint of red tint, her highlights accenting her complexion.

Dressed in jean shorts with a yellow print T-shirt, her presence gave off a very low-key air, yet she maintained an approachable personality that made meeting new people easy. People in general tended to flock toward her largely because she exuded genuineness, which was apparent in all of her friendships.

Forty-two hours later, which seemed like forever, Charmin walked into the lobby of the Beach Suite Motel. The entrance was laid out with props hinting at beach fun, such as surfboards and umbrellas. There were so many new people, both young and old, to mingle with during her ten-day stay. In the sitting area was a large-screen television that was airing a US tennis match between Steffi Graf and Martina Navratilova. The athletes were squaring off for what seemed to be an intense match. As Charmin walked toward the television, a young man crossed her path, almost as if to cut her off, but his motive was to say hello.

Charmin pondered the way he looked at her when he greeted her. The scan of his eyes pierced her as he searched her high and low with interest, not realizing their connection had only just begun. Unpacking in the room she was sharing with her sister, Charmin couldn't help but wonder who the young man was and if they would ever meet again.

Later that evening, Charmin changed into a short spaghetti-strap dress with large flowery print. With everyone dressed and ready for dinner, the family headed to a local restaurant known both for its fine dining of fresh seafood and for its live entertainment. At the center of the large dining area was a lacquered wooden dance floor. Every evening, the restaurant hosted a live band, except on Fridays, when the restaurant featured Motown sounds.

The tables were dressed with white linen. One such table, large and round, was reserved for a party of twelve and was nestled near an open window beneath a ceiling fan. The party included close relatives enjoying good eats and conversation. Everyone appeared to have ordered something different, making it easy to share the large potions that were served on a lazy Susan at the table's center.

Shortly after dinner, the room seemed to fill with more people. Charmin's family scattered to explore and mingle—and there *he* stood again, tall and handsome with a golden complexion and sexy smile. Charmin noticed the pronounced gap between his legs. People who appeared to be his friends surrounded him. Eying Charmin, he walked toward her and finally introduced himself.

"Hello, I'm Maxwell," his soft voice articulated in a Southern twang.

"Hi, I'm Charmin."

"I'm sorry about this afternoon," he said. "I didn't mean to cut you off."

Charmin smiled. "Okay."

"I live in Tampa and am just hanging out with some friends tonight." He turned and gestured toward the group of people he had been with a couple minutes ago.

"Oh, okay. I'm here with my family visiting relatives who live in the St. Petersburg area," Charmin said.

"Where are you visiting from?" Maxwell asked.

"I'm from New York City. We usually come out to the Tampa area for a week or two every summer, just before Labor Day weekend."

She pointed out family members to see if he knew any of them.

"You have a big family!" he exclaimed. This was an accurate observation, since her siblings alone constituted a party of six.

"Yes, I do have a large family," she said. "What about you?"

"My family is a party of five, which includes my parents." Maxwell smiled at Charmin.

There were good vibes all around them, so he asked her to dance, and Charmin instinctively replied, "Sure!"

They looked at each other as they moved closer, and he held his hand out to take hers, his other hand gently reaching for her waist. She lay her hand on his broad shoulder as they moved together. The world around them stood still, allowing them to become one with the sounds of Cameo.

They were inseparable, as if glued together, as they danced. When he touched her, it felt natural. They talked as if they were older and had been dating for years. She blushed with shyness as he brushed his hands along her silhouette, but she enjoyed it. They danced for what seemed like two songs before finding a bench to sit down on and get to know each other.

"I'm getting ready to start my senior year. What about you?" he asked.

"Me too—seniors!" She laughed.

"It's a cool feeling, isn't it?"

"Yes, it is," she replied. "Do you already have plans for college?"

"I do. My plans are to work in construction, but not just labor—I want to understand the engineering and blueprints and what it takes to construct something. I'll be attending a construction management trade school in Miami right after graduation. I'm trying to save as much money as I can now so I can focus solely on my studies later. Right now, I park cars at a local country club. It's pretty good, plus the tips are a bonus. What about you?" he inquired.

"Well, I don't have any master plans. I'll be attending a local state university to get a business degree. I work part time at a fast-food restaurant called Jack in the Box. It's okay. I'll say I do have a lot of fun, largely because most of my coworkers go to the same school as me," she said.

Maxwell and Charmin talked and danced until almost ten o'clock, when her family was ready to leave.

Maxwell and Charmin agreed to meet at the beach the next day. Charmin wore a one-piece black swimsuit with a deep-plunging neckline, which hinted at her full, perky breasts, giving her sexy cleavage. As she walked toward the water, Maxwell watched her, realizing he was not the only one admiring her figure. Just as she reached the water, she turned to find Maxwell behind her, smiling.

"Nice!" He grinned.

She smiled to herself, knowing he was admiring her every move.

As she allowed her toes to nestle over the coarseness of the sand and crushed shells, the coolness from the water caused her to jolt back a little. She submerged herself into the water and allowed her head to vanish under the deep blue sea, only to reappear in front of Maxwell, who was watching her, captivated.

The water began to feel surprisingly warm as her body temperature readjusted itself. Charmin enjoyed watching Maxwell swim and splash all around her, grabbing her and pulling her closely toward him. The fact that only thin layers of clothing separated their bodies created a sexual curiosity. As they played in the water, Maxwell's hands brushed against her breasts, causing her nipples to harden as he pulled her in. She felt the hardness of his phallus, and as he looked at her, she felt complete.

They played in the water for hours, chasing each other and having water fights. Before their bodies succumbed to a prune-like appearance, Maxwell offered to purchase some corndogs and soda to help replenish their thirsty bodies from the salty air. Charmin laid out a large beach towel, awaiting his return from the food stand. She watched him balance the food he had bought, noticing his effort to not drop anything in front of her.

As he approached her, she said, "I like the way you move—very impressive and good control."

He smiled. "Well, I do try to impress. Good to hear it's working," he said. "What are you doing tomorrow?"

"Nothing that I know of. I have a family function in a few days." She smiled and asked, "Why? Do you have something in mind?"

"Yes!"

"What?" she asked.

"Same place, same time."

"Okay with me!" she replied enthusiastically.

"It's a date, then," he said.

As the clock hit four, she knew it was time to head back to the motel so as not to worry her parents. The anticipation of seeing Maxwell again made leaving bearable. He offered to drive her back in his small Ford coupe, instead of her having to walk the mile and a half back to the Beach Suite Motel.

"See you tomorrow … I hope. If not, I'll understand. But I'll be there at eight in the morning either way," he promised as they sat in his car in front of the motel.

"Okay, I'll be there too," she replied as she exited his car.

Nightfall seemed different to her now. Although she was surrounded by her family, there appeared to be a void in her life, and the only explanation was that she missed seeing and talking to Maxwell. As she slept, her mind wandered, reflecting on her day at the beach. Restless and uneasy, she found her only solace in daylight. The alarm rang at seven, and its monotonous beeping caused her to leap from the bed and into the bathroom in preparation for seeing Maxwell.

She searched through her things, until she found her sexiest bathing suit. It accentuated her voluptuous, size-D breasts. Before slipping into the swimsuit, she looked at herself in the mirror to ensure she didn't need to shave. Dressed and ready to head out to the beach, she decided to jot down a note telling her family where she had gone off to so they wouldn't be alarmed or want to search for her.

A beach towel tucked into her bag, Charmin left her room wearing a sexy, net-like dress that provided very little coverage of her bathing suit. She was primarily focused on what Maxwell's reaction would be to her choice of attire. The air was hot and the sky was a beautiful bright blue—there wasn't a cloud in sight.

Just as she approached the beach entrance, she spotted Maxwell. He was sitting on a lounge chair, staring at her as she walked toward him.

"Wow!" he shouted. "I really like the way you move. You look really hot!"

"Thanks." She smiled sheepishly. "Is this your lounge chair?"

"Nope!"

"Okay. I have a beach towel we can use."

"Okay."

Charmin laid out the towel so they could lie on it before going into the water. Maxwell was already in his swim trunks, so Charmin reached for the bottom of her dress and pulled it over her head, revealing her sexy purple bathing suit. The bathing suit was similar to the black one from the previous day, except this one was backless. The style accentuated both her ass and large breasts. The day gave way to the same excitement and fun they had shared twenty-four hours prior.

After they'd played in the water for what seemed like hours, he asked her to walk with him on the beach. Maxwell reached for her hand, slightly parting his fingers to allow hers to settle in between. They strolled along the beach, holding hands as two young lovers would. As they walked together, Charmin reflected on the fun days they had shared, and then she laid her head on Maxwell's shoulder as he embraced her tightly.

The following day, they met at a local music store. They rummaged through the selections of Motown hits in search of Cameo until Maxwell finally found one of their records.

"Now we'll always have the song 'Sparkles' to remind us of our union," he said.

They walked hand in hand along the boulevard, admiring the ocean view, and Maxwell suddenly, yet gently, pushed Charmin to the side, as if to tell her something. His hands had a firm grip around her waist, and he eyed her before saying, "Can I ask you a personal question?"

She responded, "Sure. What?"

He hesitated for a moment and then asked, "Can I kiss you?"

When he asked this question, Charmin was too preoccupied gazing into his light brown eyes, so she had to reflect on what he had asked. Once she realized, her facial expression changed and she nodded a yes. The two of them moved closer to each other, as if in slow motion. She stood at 5'4 and he at 5'10, so he leaned into her. As they stared into one another's eyes, their lips gently touched.

The heat from their lips caused them to tighten their embrace, and their lips locked in a passionate, yet soft, kiss.

"Thank you. That was the first kiss that really meant something to me. I've kissed others, but there is something about you that feels right," he said between kisses. "Are you busy this evening? I'd like to take you out for pizza."

"I'll have to check with my family to be sure they didn't already make plans."

"Okay."

"But yes! I'd liked to have pizza with you," she said.

"It's almost three o'clock. Do you want me to drop you off so you can spend time with your family? We'll see each other tonight, as long as it's okay with them."

"That's a good idea! What time, and where should we meet?"

"How about six this evening? I'll pick you up from the motel," he said.

"Okay, that sounds good," she said as they walked toward his compact Ford coupe en route to the motel.

Charmin contemplated how to approach her parents so as not to cause too much of a commotion. As she exited Maxwell's car, she leaned back and smiled at him. "See ya later."

As she walked toward the entrance of the motel, she looked back at Maxwell. She saw that he was watching her walk away, which made her smile to herself.

Her parents' offered their consent, so Charmin bustled around her room, trying to decide what to wear on her first real date with Maxwell. Finally, she decided on a denim miniskirt, a sleeveless button blouse, and sandals.

Every time she glanced at the clock, it appeared stuck on the same time, so she decided to walk down to the lobby. Charmin hung around the pool near the entrance of the lobby so she could see Maxwell drive up. *Only forty minutes to go,* she thought to herself as intimate feelings invaded her mind. She tried to keep her composure as his gray coupe pulled up at the entryway, and then she dashed toward the lobby to greet him.

Maxwell pulled up to the curb and stepped out of the car. He searched for Charmin only to see her heading toward him, smiling. His face lit up with excitement.

As she approached him, he smiled and said, "Hey! You look good."

"Thanks," she said.

"How long can you stay out?" Maxwell inquired.

"They didn't say. They just said to be safe and have fun—but not too much fun! Oh, and not to forget the key to my room. So no curfew," she said, smiling. "How long would you like us to hang out?"

"Not too late. I just wanted to know."

"Okay," she said.

"Ready?"

"Yes," Charmin replied.

Watching her every move, Maxwell reached for the passenger door to allow Charmin to enter his car. As Charmin sat, her miniskirt seemed to retract up her thighs, creating a micro miniskirt effect, which enticed Maxwell.

"Nice," he said.

As the car pulled away, Maxwell asked, "Have you eaten at Uno's before?"

"No," she said. "But I've played Uno, the card game!" They both laughed.

"It serves really good pizza."

"Okay, sounds good to me," she responded.

The night air was like a silk blanket wrapping around her soft skin. As they crossed the bridge into Tampa, Charmin admired all the lights around the popular city. The restaurant was spacious and crowded, but the mood was light and fun. Seated at a booth, they conversed about everything from school to future aspirations.

Maxwell took the liberty to order for them—a sausage and pepperoni pizza and chocolate milkshakes.

After dinner, Maxwell said, "It's eight. I'd like to show you my favorite hangout spot, if you are interested."

"I'm interested! If you like it, I'm sure I will too."

The car was headed in the direction of the Tampa airport. Maxwell veered off to a remote road, which ended at an open field, providing a spectacular view of the airport. They watched approaching aircrafts towering overhead and could hear the landing gears project out.

The atmosphere created such a romantic setting. It seemed wasteful for them not to succumb to their physical urges, so Maxwell asked for a kiss. Charmin turned to face Maxwell. She realized that the boundaries that had restricted them at the beach no longer existed. Kissing fostered a new feeling of intimacy and passion between them. He touched her intimately for the first time, and she touched him.

He unfastened her blouse, exposing her bra and voluptuous breasts, and she unzipped his pants, exposing his manhood. They examined each other while satisfying their sexual curiosity.

At just past midnight, Maxwell pulled up to the motel to drop Charmin off.

"I want to see you again," he said.

She responded, "Me too. Can you come by a little early I'd like to introduce you to my family if that's okay?"

"Sure."

So they planned to meet for lunch near the beach around one in the afternoon the next day.

Because Charmin was spending a lot of time with Maxwell, her parents grew concerned about her whereabouts. So Charmin was glad she asked Maxwell to come to the motel before lunch so she could introduce him to her family. Charmin waited near the entrance for Maxwell to pull up. It was just past eleven thirty as his car drove up to the entrance, where Charmin was waiting for him. Dressed in a casual dress shirt with jeans and sneakers, he exited his Ford coupe and greeted Charmin with a kiss hello. After meeting her family, Maxwell was instantly inducted into her family circle.

After the introduction, Maxwell asked Charmin's parents if it would be okay for him to take Charmin to a local café for lunch. Charmin was impressed with his respect for her parents and family. She realized he was going to be more than just a "summer fling." They held hands as they headed for the café across the street from the beach.

At the café, they were seated outside at a small, round table with a view of the beach. As they sat enjoying the view, out-of-the-blue, Maxwell turned to Charmin and said, "I really like you."

Chapter 2

Charmin was not as surprised because the feeling was mutual. "I like you too," she responded.

"I've never had a long-distance relationship before—I have only dated locally—but I am willing to give this a chance. It is going to be hard not being able to see you when I want, but I guess we can call each other often and write. What do you think?" he said.

"This is pretty new for me, too. I've never really dated anyone. I've had some admirers before, and gone on dates to the movies or bowling, but nothing really serious. I think you are pretty special and would like to try this with you," she said.

Maxwell smiled and reached for her hands across the table. As the waiter approached, Maxwell said, "I've never eaten here before, but I hear they have good burgers. Do you want to try one?"

"Sure, I like hamburgers," she responded.

Maxwell ordered two cheeseburgers with a side of fries and iced tea.

"I have a family function tomorrow, which may take all day. My parents and close family friends rented a sailboat for the day, and we're going sailing around Tampa. Afterward, we'll probably have a family dinner. Would you like to come?" Charmin asked.

"Sure! What time tomorrow?"

"Can I call you later? Right now I don't know what the plan is."

"Okay, here is my number."

Charmin searched her handbag for a pen. Maxwell got up, walked toward the waiter stand, and asked for a pen, and as he was returning, Charmin just smiled because words weren't needed.

Maxwell reached for the phone pad in her hands and said, "Where would you like me to write it?"

"Anywhere under the 'M' heading is fine," she said.

Maxwell proceeded to write his name, address, and phone number in her little phone pad. Once he was done, he handed the pad back to her. After she glanced over his contact information, she flipped to the last page, ripped out a sheet of paper, and wrote her contact information for him. She handed him the sheet once she had finished and said, "Now we can reach each other, by both phone and mail."

After lunch, they walked along the sidewalk before heading back to the motel. It was almost two thirty in the afternoon, and Maxwell said he had to go.

"I'm meeting some of my friends this afternoon—the ones that you saw me with the first night we met. They want to hang out since I've been spending so much time with you. They feel a little neglected."

At the entrance of the motel, he gave her a bear hug and a kiss so everyone could see they were together. As he headed back to his car, he shouted, "Hey, don't forget to call me later about what time I need to meet you and your family tomorrow. I can't wait to see you again, baby!"

After conversing with her family, Charmin got the okay for Maxwell to participate in the family outing. Both of her parents were loving and fair, within reason, like most parents. She searched through her phonebook to obtain Maxwell's contact information before calling his house.

As the phone rang, Charmin's nerves surfaced. Before she could calm them, a woman answered—Maxwell's mother. Her voice was very pleasant as she said he was not home yet and asked if she could take a message. Charmin felt at ease and provided his mother with the time and place for Maxwell to meet her the following day. Then she thanked his mom for taking the message before saying good-bye.

The alarm rang at five thirty the next morning. Charmin's parents wanted everyone up and at breakfast no later than seven o'clock. The motel had a small restaurant that served a continental-style breakfast and featured a hot waffle maker. Charmin enjoyed fresh waffles anytime she had the opportunity.

By eight, everyone was ready to head out to the marina for some sailing. Maxwell was parking his car as Charmin and her family left the motel. A chartered shuttle bus was waiting to take them all to the marina and back.

The marina was crowded with both people and boats. As the captain called, "All aboard," they all got on deck to wave off as the boat debarked from port. They set sail into the open sea with the wind at their backs. The adventure of sailing was underway.

Around six in the evening, the shuttle bus returned to the motel. After having such a grand time on the open sea, everyone was exhausted and hungry. Maxwell didn't want to intrude, so he said, "Maybe I should go—I don't want your family to feel like I've just inserted myself."

Before Charmin could respond, her mother called her over and said, "He seems like a nice young man. Be sure to ask him to stay for dinner."

Charmin turned and looked at Maxwell with a loving smile and said, "Well, looks like my parents really like you and would like if you stayed for dinner. No intrusion here!"

The restaurant was close, so everyone agreed to walk. Dinner was as fun and relaxing as the day on the sailboat had been. Everyone seemed to be having a wonderful time feasting on seafood. Maxwell conversed with Charmin's family and friends as if they'd known him for a long time.

Maxwell mentioned to Charmin's family that there was going to be a concert at a nearby park in two days and asked if anyone was interested in attending. Everyone at the table seemed pleased, and he said he would obtain more information and get back to them.

After leaving the restaurant, they walked back toward the motel, noticing through their fatigue the star-studded night sky. Maxwell said good night and thanked the family as he took Charmin's hand and led her toward his car.

Leaning against his car, he said, "I had a lot of fun today. Thank you for inviting me and letting me participate in your family outing. I'll call you sometime tomorrow with the information about the concert. I'd really like to take you, even if your family decides not to attend. I hope they do decide to go—they'll enjoy it."

"Thanks. I'd like to go with you," she said.

Maxwell reached forward and planted a wet and passionate kiss against her lips. Their passion led to a little French kissing. Charmin found it difficult to say good-bye before Maxwell entered his car and drove home.

The motel phone rang at noon the next day. Maxwell was calling to give her the information about the outdoor concert. Knowing they would not see each other that day, they talked for hours. When she hung up, her ear was hot from having the receiver rest against it for such a long period. The day seemed empty without Maxwell there, and even her parents inquired about his whereabouts.

At five the following evening, Maxwell drove to the motel to pick up Charmin for the concert, only to discover her family had decided to attend as well. They all headed to the nearby park where the Whispers danced and sang on an outdoor stage. They almost met Prince, who made a guest appearance, but a large crowd had gathered, making him too difficult to meet. The family and the couple were only able to see him from a distance.

Maxwell enjoyed spending time with Charmin's family, and they apparently enjoyed having him around, which made their union easy.

In less than two days, Charmin and her family would be heading back to New York City. Maxwell was invited to dinner with her family again. This time, they chose a restaurant on Anna Maria Island along a pier overlooking the ocean.

At the restaurant, in front of Charmin's family, Maxwell gave her a square box from a local jewelry shop and asked her to open it. Inside was a beautiful sterling silver cross necklace, which he helped put around her neck.

Charmin said, "Oh, how beautiful! Thank you so much. I love it!"

Maxwell just smiled, knowing he had done well. Charmin's family shared comments about what a nice gift it was and how they made a nice couple. Charmin and Maxwell cuddled near each other on the drive back to the motel.

Charmin's family was leaving at two in the morning on Sunday. Maxwell wanted to see her again before she left, so he asked if he could come by on Saturday, which would give them time to relax and hang around the pool before she had to leave for New York.

The motel had a small seating area surrounding the pool. They lounged near the water, sharing a recliner and exchanging plans to meet for each other's prom and graduation. Just past seven in the evening, Maxwell gave Charmin a bear hug and passionate kiss good-bye.

"I'll write you and call," he said.

"Me too," she replied.

On the long drive back to New York City, all Charmin could think about was this great guy she had encountered. She reflected on how they had moved as one during the entire Tampa visit. She somehow felt different feelings of intimacy and a new sense of sexuality and wondered how a person could have such an impact on her life in such a short amount of time. This gave her somewhat looming thoughts. They had agreed to write letters to each other weekly and to talk as often as permitted, which comforted her.

She found herself gazing out the window, reflecting on the way Maxwell looked and how he had held her with such strength. His voice was incredibly sexy to her, as was his smile, and she recounted everything he had said to her. She smiled to herself as she remembered. Recalling the feeling of his lips against hers created wetness between her thighs.

Forty-two hours later, Charmin was lying in her own bed, writing her first letter to Maxwell and entertaining naughty fantasies. She decided to perfume the letter to remind him of what she smelled like. At a little after one o'clock, sleep swept over her, her thoughts still centered on Maxwell.

The aroma of flapjacks and bacon woke Charmin up at ten thirty the next morning. As she stepped out of bed and went into the bathroom, it occurred to her that she needed to visit the post office. Her first letter was ready to be mailed, although she did wonder if Maxwell had written his.

Charmin grabbed a cup of orange juice, folded a flapjack, placed a bacon strip in the middle, and headed out of the door to her Nissan Sentra.

While driving she rolled down the window to welcome the cool fall air. Charmin felt a sense of seriousness about herself, normally she would brush things off but today she took note of her feelings. Maxwell had touched her in a way unfamiliar to her regular encounters. She couldn't stop thinking about him and how he made her feel. Cupid found his way into her heart.

A few days later, she received a letter from Maxwell. Then, a week later, Charmin received a phone call from him, which would become a regular occurrence.

"I've got it," Charmin called out as the phone rang. "Hello?"

"Hi, Charmin."

"Hi, Maxwell, I was just thinking about you. How are you doing?"

"I'm doing well, thanks. How are you doing?"

"Better now," she responded.

"I just wanted to hear your voice and let you know I was thinking about you. That's all. I'm going fishing with some friends. Just wanted to say hello."

"Thanks for the call, and have fun fishing. I'm heading to the mall with some friends too."

"Okay. Talk to you soon."

"Okay. Bye," she said

Their phone conversations normally lasted well through the night or morning. They realized they had so much to say to each other, and phone conversations were not enough; they couldn't wait to reunite.

It wasn't until five months later that they were able to see each other again. This time, Charmin traveled alone to attend her cousin Mildred's wedding in Atlanta, Georgia. Mildred blocked thirty rooms for her family and the wedding party. Charmin's flight arrived in Atlanta late Friday night.

The wedding was being held at the Omni Hotel. Her cousin's guest list topped 150 people, including her wedding party of twenty-four. The ceremony was scheduled for Monday evening at six. This was appreciated by her fiancé, since it was the day after Super Bowl XXIII.

Maxwell had to work late Friday night, so the couple agreed he would travel to Atlanta on Saturday afternoon. The hotel was about forty minutes from the airport, so Maxwell took a cab. Charmin had a large bedroom to herself, which she was happy to share.

Knowing what time his flight was scheduled to land, Charmin headed down to the lobby, encountering several family members just lounging around.

"Hey, Charmin!" her cousin Sarah said. "I was going to call you. We are all heading downtown for dinner."

Charmin knew in her heart that she really didn't want to go, but she also didn't want to offend her cousin by saying no. After all, not only had Sarah invited her, but she had even talked Charmin's parents into letting her come out to Atlanta alone.

"Well, I'm waiting on my friend to arrive. His flight landed an hour ago, so I'm sure he's en route, and he'll be hungry. Can we wait for him to get in so we can all travel together?" she asked.

"Sure! We have two rented shuttle buses that will accommodate fifty people per bus. Is he coming by taxi?"

"Yes."

"Okay."

Less than ten minutes later, Charmin noticed a young, handsome guy walking through the revolving doors of the hotel. Maxwell glanced around and spotted her on a sofa chair looking at him. They exchanged smiles before she walked toward him and embraced him.

"Hi. How was your flight?"

"Hey. It was good. I'm really happy to see you again."

"Yeah, me too! Let me introduce you to some of my family members. Oh, and they want us to go out to dinner. Is that okay? Are you hungry?"

"That's fine. I am a little hungry."

Charmin introduced Maxwell to about thirty-five people, some friends and some family. She walked toward Sarah and said, "I'm going to take him upstairs so he can drop off his bags, and then we'll be right back."

"Okay. We'll see you in about ten minutes, all right?"

"Absolutely!"

Maxwell and Charmin walked hand in hand toward the elevators. A group of people were already waiting, so the couple decided to wait for the next one to have more privacy. A chiming sound rang out as the doors opened.

Maxwell stepped in first, and Charmin followed. Before the doors closed, he planted a kiss on her lips.

"I've missed you so much. It's crazy," he said.

"I know. Talking to you on the phone helps, but seeing you in person is so much better," she said.

They embraced each other tightly as the elevator climbed to the eighth floor. As they walked toward their room, Charmin started to feel shy and nervous, knowing they not only were alone but would also be sharing a room and a bed.

Maxwell noticed Charmin's uneasiness and said, "I care about you a lot, and I don't want to rush anything between us, okay?"

"Thank you," she answered.

She reached for the key, which was wedged deep in her pocket, and then inserted it into the slot, allowing the light to turn green. The door opened to a spacious room with a large, queen-size bed.

"Okay. Let me drop my luggage here because your family is waiting on us," Maxwell said as he placed his bags against the left side of the bed. He reached for Charmin's hand before exiting the room.

Chapter 3

The couple reached the lobby as everyone was boarding the shuttle. "Hey, you guys. I'm glad you were able to make the bus. We are heading downtown to Ruth Chris," the driver said.

The restaurant was beautifully decorated, and the view of downtown Atlanta was spectacular. As everybody disembarked, a hostess greeted them and asked everyone to follow her into a reserved room. The room was set up like a large "T" and sat about thirty-five people comfortably. All the food was already set out in a nice display. The table was flush against the wall in a buffet style with a few waiters on hand. The evening was lively and incredibly loud, filled with laughter and conversation.

Throughout the evening, Charmin watched Maxwell savor the taste of liquor and beer. As young adults, they enjoyed embracing their sense of freedom to explore new things.

"Hey, what are you drinking?"

"Hey, babe. This is called a Long Island iced tea. It's pretty good—not as good as my creation, but acceptable," he replied.

"What's in it?"

"Well, as a bartender, I can tell you it's made with a shot of gin, tequila, Captain Morgan rum, vodka, triple sec, and sour mix, plus I would add a shot of lime juice," he explained, grinning.

"Can I have a little sip?" she asked.

"No way! Sharing a man's drink requires something in return. What will you give me if I share my drink with you?" He smiled at her.

"I don't know. What would you like?" she asked, staring into his eyes.

"I'll be happy with a kiss."

"I can handle that." She leaned forward and planted a wet kiss over his lips.

"Nice," he said. He proceeded to share his drink with her.

At around eleven that evening, the shuttle bus returned to the hotel, and everyone said good night as they all headed to their rooms. Maxwell and Charmin walked slowly toward the elevator while leaning against each other. Once they arrived in the room, Maxwell indicated that he wanted to take a shower after his long trip.

Charmin drew the quilt off the bed and folded it at the base. She rummaged through her luggage in search of a cute set of pajamas. As she undressed, she could hear Maxwell humming in the shower. The white tee and mini tri-colored shorts were made of cotton and felt soft against her skin.

Unsure how to position herself on the bed, Charmin felt her nerves getting the best of her again. The bathroom door opened, and Maxwell stood in the doorway, shirtless and in fitted shorts. He looked at Charmin and then flipped the light switch.

He walked toward the bed. "You look beautiful."

"Thank you."

He reached the bed, leaning toward the nightstand and clicking that light off too. Charmin could feel the weight shift as he situated himself on the bed and reached for her.

Maxwell's body felt hard and warm as Charmin lost herself in his arms. He kissed her on the forehead and said, "Let's get some sleep. I'm pretty beat. Good night, baby."

"Good night."

Charmin was relieved that Maxwell respected her enough to wait until she was ready. They slept in each other's arms as the night turned into day.

Sunday morning brought new feelings of intimacy as they awoke near each other. The sunlight made Charmin's tee-top sheer, revealing her nipples and areolae. Maxwell's facial expression revealed that he was very turned on.

"You are such a beautiful and sexy woman. I feel like I can just lose myself in you. What an erogenous feeling." He recommended getting some breakfast as a distraction. "It's almost ten in the morning. I could drink a cold glass of orange juice right now," he said.

"Okay. I'll go take a shower," she answered.

Charmin got out of bed and walked past Maxwell, sensing his eyes on her. She closed the door to the bathroom and stared in the mirror for a while, knowing he was in the next room. As she started to undress, she felt wetness between her thighs; her short tricolor shorts had a wet spot.

"I want him, but I'm so afraid. I don't know what to do with all of these erotic feelings," she said to herself.

Showered, a towel wrapped around her body, she opened the bathroom door. As she walked past Maxwell again, she knew he was watching her, so she looked at him. His eyes were wide and focused on her, but she kept her cool. Instead, she started to go through her luggage in search of something to wear. She reached for a purple matching bra and panty set.

"Wow. Those are nice. I like the color purple. Would you wear those for me?" he asked.

"Okay. I will, just for you."

Maxwell sat up on the bed and said, "I guess I should go get cleaned up so you can get dressed."

"That would be really nice," she replied.

As Maxwell elevated himself from the bed, his fitted shorts displayed a very large, bulky shape. "Down, boy, down. It can't help itself!" He smiled as he walked toward the bathroom and grabbed his carry-on bag.

She contemplated her clothing options. She looked out the window to assess the weather. It was January, and Atlanta was experiencing temperatures in the midfifties, so she reached for a long skirt and sweater that would look fantastic with her vintage calf-length boots. While brushing her hair and applying light makeup to her face, Charmin knew in her heart that she wanted her first experience to be with Maxwell.

Sexual feelings kept running through her mind. Charmin was already on the pill due to heavy menstrual flow, so the possibility of getting pregnant was not as worrisome as that of contracting a sexually transmitted disease. Charmin had no idea how many women, or what kinds of women, Maxwell had already been with. They would have to take their conversation to the next level if sex was going to play a part in their relationship.

The bathroom doors opened and Maxwell walked out already dressed. He looked at her and said, "I'm a pretty lucky guy to have found such a beautiful person." He walked toward her and reached for her hand. Her hand resting in his, he kissed the back of her hand and said, "Are you ready to get something to eat? I'm pretty hungry both for you and for food."

"I'm ready."

He walked ahead and stopped at the closet to grab her coat and his jacket. Like a gentleman, he helped her with her coat and kissed the back of her neck. She buttoned her leather jacket and reached to pull her gloves from her pocket. When she turned to face the door, Maxwell leaned against her and kissed her on the lips. He wrapped his arm around her and held her in a tight embrace as she reciprocated his advances.

"I've never said this to anyone before, but … I think I love you." The air in the room evaporated at once as he spoke.

"No one has ever said that to me before. Thank you. I think I love you too," she responded.

"I want to be with you, but I want you to be comfortable and ready. I've never slept with anyone before. I know I'm eighteen and still a virgin; I've been waiting for you, apparently. No pressure. I just wanted to share my feelings with you."

"I've never been with anyone, either, and have never really thought about it until now. I'm attracted to you, and these feelings of intimacy just keep invading my thoughts."

"Really? Nice to know that. So ... what kinds of intimate thoughts, exactly? Care to share?" he asked, curious.

"No. Not yet," she said, smiling.

"Okay, okay. Let's go get something to eat," he said.

Chapter 4

Charmin and Maxwell headed out the door with no real plan in mind. Reaching the lobby, they took in the grand entrance and knew a restaurant or two had to be nestled somewhere in the hotel. As they were searching for restaurants, they saw Charmin's cousin, Mildred, who had just come from the salon with a group of friends. They were also in search of food. It was almost noon, and they had been getting their hair and nails done since nine that morning.

"Hey, you guys. What's up? I am so hungry. Have you eaten yet?" Mildred asked.

"No. We were just looking for a restaurant; we can smell food. We are not sure where the scent is coming from," Charmin replied.

"It's Sunday, so the Prime Meridian serves brunch until two in the afternoon. It is just down this hallway—follow us," Mildred said.

The restaurant was full of people walking around with plates of food. Mildred flagged to some friends who were sitting at a large, round table. Before sitting down, Maxwell motioned to Charmin to go look at the spread of food.

"This is quite a feast. I'm hungry, but not that hungry," he said, laughing.

"Yeah. I know what you mean. It's almost too much food at one time," she said.

Maxwell placed his arm around Charmin's waist and walked to the line of people waiting to get food.

"What do you want to eat?" he asked.

"I'm not sure; everything looks good. I think maybe a waffle, some bacon, and the fruit medley."

"That sounds good! Hmm … I'm thinking a waffle, some bacon, and eggs along with hash browns definitely sounds good. Oh, plus I'd like a large glass of orange juice," he stated.

The table was filled with food and empty plates as the waitress tried to clear off the table. During brunch, a friend of Mildred's had invited everyone to join him and his family at a nearby sports bar to watch the Super Bowl. The sports club had billiard tables, dartboards, and three large-screen televisions to enjoy the game.

Maxwell helped Charmin with her coat. Then he pulled the chair out to allow her to position herself to sit. She noticed she was being watched by family and friends already seated at the table.

"You guys make a nice couple. Oh, to be young again," someone said.

Maxwell and Charmin smiled at each other and gave a general word of thanks to the table. After breakfast, everyone wondered aloud what they would do for the remainder of the day. The idea of the sports bar was definitely part of the plan, but the game didn't start until after four, and it was only a quarter until two.

The shuttle bus was able to drop off and pick up, so they decided collectively to head to the mall before meeting at the sports bar.

As they headed toward the shuttle bus, Maxwell whispered in Charmin's ear, "I can't stop thinking about you in that wet towel this morning. You turn me on so much."

Charmin smiled. "You turn me on, too."

As they boarded the bus, Maxwell reached to give her his

hands to support her weight as she stepped upward. They found a seat together and cuddled near each other while looking out the window. The bus driver reminded everyone of the time to be at the pick-up point.

Fifteen minutes later, the shuttle bus pulled up to the mall, and the bus driver, once again, reminded everyone of the pick-up time. Everyone seemed to head in different directions in a hurry. Maxwell reached for Charmin's hand as they walked amiably around the mall. They walked into different clothing stores to get a sense of what the other liked. Maxwell was a jeans-and-dress-shirt type of guy, whereas Charmin enjoyed skirts and dresses. As they walked past a shoe store, Charmin motioned Maxwell to stop.

The store was stacked with designer shoes and boots, which caught Charmin's attention. She eyed three-inch high-heeled chocolate suede shoes that matched her long, cream-colored skirt. Maxwell could see the excitement on her face and asked her to try them on.

Seeing her walk around in the three-inch heels enticed him enough to say, "I'd like to buy those for you, if you really like them. I think they look pretty sexy on your feet."

"Really?! You would buy these for me? Wow, no guy has ever purchased shoes for me before."

"Then let me be the first."

Charmin removed the shoes and proceeded to put on her boots.

"No, wait. Why don't you wear the new ones instead?" he proposed.

"That's a good idea," she said.

She flagged a salesperson to explain her intent, placed her boots in the box, and kept her new heels on. As Maxwell paid at the register, her feelings for him seemed to get deeper each time she looked at him. She walked alongside him and reached for his hand as he carried her shopping bag.

It was almost four, and the driver had asked everyone to be at the pick-up point soon, so they started for the main entrance of the mall so as not to be late. Everyone was present as the shuttle bus pulled up and opened its doors. Almost everyone was carrying a bag or two, validating that going to the mall was a good idea.

The driver ensured everyone with a shopping bag that the bags would be safe if left tucked under the bus seats. Maxwell put his arms around Charmin as the bus headed to the sports bar, Dantanna's, which was bustling with people sitting around and socializing.

Seated around three tables was a crowd of people who appeared to be Charmin's family and their friends. Before joining them, Maxwell asked Charmin for a kiss and said, "I'm having the best time, and you look pretty hot in those sexy heels."

"Thank you. I'm having a good time too."

"Would you like to play pool when a table is free?"

"Okay."

As they waited for the table, Charmin turned to Maxwell and said, "I'm ready."

Unsure what she was referring to, he said, "I'm a 49ers fan. This is going to be an exciting game. I'm ready for it to begin already too."

"No. I mean—*I'm ready.*"

"Okay," he said. It took Maxwell ten minutes to understand what Charmin was referring to before he turned and looked at her to ask, *"What?"*

Charmin realized he finally understood what she was trying to say to him without being too forward. "I'm feeling comfortable and a little warm all over."

"Really? Nice. Do you want to go now?"

"No. Let's wait until after the game, okay?"

"This is going to be a long game for me now. You have made me so happy. Thank you."

Maxwell couldn't focus on the game. Although he enjoyed being there, he really wanted to be back in the hotel with Charmin. He kept looking at her to see if she was playing with him or if she was genuinely ready. Maxwell reached for her hand and held it securely in his own.

"I love you, Charmin," he said.

"I love you too, Maxwell."

Although the game was lively, it was too long for both Maxwell and Charmin. They rushed past many people heading back to the bus. Maxwell could not keep his hands off Charmin as he teased her playfully.

Once on the bus, they situated themselves near the back and engaged in passionate kissing. The bus driver's voice startled them as he asked everyone to collect their belongings before exiting the bus. Charmin reminded Maxwell of her boot bag, which was somewhere near the center under a seat, and Maxwell finally found it after a few minutes of searching.

Exiting, they thanked everyone and, in a hurried motion, headed for the elevator. Maxwell could not keep his hands off her body. Once they reached the room, Charmin surrendered herself to Maxwell. Their bodies submersed in the act of ecstasy as they embraced their desires.

The hotel phone rang at ten the next morning. It was Sarah calling to inform the couple that she wanted her family and friends to attend Mildred and Jeff's wedding brunch. Maxwell, who had answered the phone, confirmed their attendance. After doing so, he kissed Charmin good morning.

Kissing and touching each other gave way to erotic feelings, and Maxwell uttered, "I didn't know your body could make me feel this way. I can't get enough of you. Baby, I love you. Thank you."

"What a rush of energy! I've never experienced anything like that before. I liked it a lot. Want to do it again?" she said as she planted a kiss on his lips before saying, "I love you too, Maxwell."

"Anything you want, babe."

She allowed him to insert his thick, long shaft inside her tight, wet canal again. They engaged in the art of lovemaking before dressing.

Brunch lasted for two hours, followed by the women getting massages and the guys playing racquetball. At four, the photographers were scheduled to take group photos of the wedding party and family. The ceremony started promptly at six in the evening. Maxwell and

Charmin danced and socialized until eleven before heading back to their room, where Maxwell made love to her repeatedly.

During the night, as they lay in each other's arms, Maxwell and Charmin conversed about their future.

"Can you believe we'll be graduating in a few months? High school graduates—wow! I feel like we can take on the world, just the two of us. I am scheduled to attend a construction management trade school in September. When do you start at SUNY?" he asked.

"I'll be starting in August. I hate that we are leaving tomorrow. I'm going to miss you so much more now."

"I'll miss you too, but we'll see each other again. We'll need to make plans to attend each other's proms, and then graduation in June. I have to attend a training seminar in July, so let's plan to meet in New York, okay?"

"Okay, that's great! I'm looking forward to that visit."

Sleep swept over them as they cuddled.

Their flights were leaving around the same time, so they said good-bye to everyone before heading to the airport in a cab. They lounged together until boarding was announced, and then they said good-bye with a passionate kiss.

Maxwell called later that afternoon, and they talked for hours, reminiscing about their visit in Atlanta. Charmin knew in her heart that she had found the man she wanted to share her life with. Maxwell was not like any guy she had ever been with, because he touched her soul. They continued to talk and write letters to fill the gap between them. Charmin had the opportunity to see Maxwell again in April while attending her cousin's surprise birthday party in Tampa.

Maxwell arrived at the airport around nine in the morning to take Charmin to her cousin's house. The party was on track for seven, but Maxwell was scheduled to work until nine that evening. On the drive to her cousin's house, Maxwell asked Charmin if she knew how to drive a manual car because his Ford coupe was a stick shift.

"No. Is it hard?"

"No, not really. Once you do it, it gets pretty easy and fun actually. Would you like to try it?"

"I'm a little nervous. I don't want to damage your car."

"Oh, you won't. It's okay. From where you are sitting, just listen to the sound of the engine. When the sound goes into a low mode, it means the car needs power, and when it's high or there's a screeching sound, that is when you retract the gear."

With his foot placed on the clutch, he allowed Charmin to shift gears as he drove.

"This stick shift is pretty hard to shift into gear," she commented.

"You can handle anything you put your mind to. It's pretty easy. You can handle this stick; just relax. Listen to the engine and have fun. I'll do the rest."

They both looked at each other, reminiscing about their last sexual encounter.

"Can we have sex tonight? I've been thinking about you a lot and cannot wait to put my hard dick inside your tight, wet pussy," he looked at her hungrily.

"Yes, we can have sex. I've missed you too."

Maxwell leaned forward and kissed Charmin.

Later that evening, Maxwell joined Charmin at the party. After a long day of parking cars and bartending, he was ready for some relaxation. Searching for her among the crowd of people dancing and conversing, he finally found his woman. She was wearing a short, white halter dress, which crossed around her neckline, creating a peekaboo opening between her large, perky breasts.

The moment Maxwell laid eyes on her, his cock grew in size. Watching her move around while he admired her body excited him. He could not wait to be near her and possess what he believed was now his. He moved through the crowd toward her, scanning her body. He reached out to her, and she received his hands.

"Hello, beautiful. You look amazing," he said, continuing to look her up and down.

"Thank you. I bought this just for you," she said, smiling at him.

"My dick is rock-hard because of you in that sexy dress. Can you see the bulge against my pants?" he whispered.

"Yes. I do see a very large object against your thighs," she whispered, looking around to make sure no one was listening.

"Please don't think I'm crazy, but I need you right now, or I may cum in my pants."

"Right now?! How? Where?"

"Follow me. I saw a closet on the main floor when I arrived. Everyone is downstairs, so we may have some privacy on the main floor. Is that okay?"

"Closet ... okay."

Holding Charmin's hand, Maxwell discreetly walked back upstairs to the main area. There was a narrow coat closet nestled in a corner away from the main traffic area. He proceeded to open the closet doors, but stopped as they heard voices approaching.

"I think they are gone now. Sounds like they went outside. Coast is clear," Charmin said.

"Cool!" Maxwell whispered anxiously.

Maxwell opened the closet doors and shuffled a few coats and jackets to one side. That allowed them ample space to stand as he reached for Charmin to join him inside the closet. In semidarkness, Maxwell pulled Charmin's body tightly to his. They engaged in heated kissing and groping.

"My dick is so hard. I need to take it out of my pants."

Maxwell unzipped his pants to free his hard, thick shaft. Charmin grabbed a hold of it and started stroking his throbbing cock, causing pre-love juice to form along her grip with each vigorous stroke.

"Is your pussy wet?" Maxwell asked as he eyed her with lust.

"Touch me and find out," Charmin teased.

"Nice," he reached his hand under her dress, and between her thighs he felt moisture against her panties. "You are nice and wet, just like I remember."

As he stroked against her panties, Charmin was becoming aroused and started to breathe heavily. Maxwell brushed her panties to the side with his hand, and then inserted two fingers insider her wet, hot pussy. Enjoying his movements, Charmin spread her legs wider to accept his thick fingers inside of her.

Maxwell pressed his lips into Charmin's, and they French kissed while masturbating each other. The intensity peaked when Maxwell climaxed against Charmin's hands and his pants and nectar juice poured out of Charmin onto Maxwell's hand.

"That was amazing! Baby, thank you. That was so hot and crazy good."

"I liked it a lot. I feel so free and relaxed at the same time," she responded. "Do you think anyone heard us?"

"I don't think so. Let's get out of here before someone does."

"Okay. Let's stop by the bathroom. My hands are wet and sticky," she said, staring at Maxwell.

"My hands feel silky wet from your pussy juice. I like it, but washing our hands is probably a good idea."

After cleaning up in the bathroom, Charmin and Maxwell rejoined the party and danced until two in the morning. Charmin's short visit proved another incredible experience between her and Maxwell.

After graduation, as planned, Maxwell had to attend a construction training seminar at the Jarvis center in New York. Charmin met him at the train station after the seminar was over. They couldn't believe almost three weeks had gone by since they had last seen each other, but nothing had changed between them. Maxwell wrapped his arms around Charmin as he kissed her hello.

"I'd like to introduce you to some of my friends, if you are up for it," she said.

"Sure, I'm game," he responded.

Charmin decided to take him to South Street Sea Port, Pier 16 because his hotel was near downtown. The pier was bustling with people who were enjoying the warm weather. The restaurants located at the pier were known for their cocktails and superb cuisine. The pier overlooked the Hudson River and featured a view of the Brooklyn

Bridge adorned with lights, providing a spectacular, romantic setting for lovers at the pier.

Charmin went in search of a pay phone located near the entrance of the restaurant and called her friends to let them know they would be at Stella's, a restaurant on the pier and to invite them to join Maxwell and her for drinks.

A few minutes later, a cluster of friends arrived to meet Maxwell and welcome him into their circle. Maxwell established a tab with the bartender, which Charmin found interesting as the drinks started to flow freely. After two hours and a couple of martinis, Sam Adams, Coors, and vodka shots, the bill totaled eighty dollars, which Maxwell volunteered to pay. Everyone thanked Maxwell, who seemed to be a hit with her friends as they said good-bye.

"That was incredibly generous of you to pay the full bill. My friends are all working and would have paid for their own drinks. But thank you anyway." Without hesitation, she kissed Maxwell on the cheek.

"It's my pleasure, babe. I don't mind, especially since they are good friends of yours—soon to be mine." He smiled and accepted her kiss.

As the couple walked along the pier, Maxwell noticed a vendor selling flowers. He asked Charmin what her favorite flowers were, and she responded, "Red roses and calla lilies."

So Maxwell purchased a dozen red roses and calla lilies for his best girl.

"Thank you. I love them, and I love you."

"I love you too. Anything for my girl."

After a light dinner, they hailed a cab to go back to Maxwell's hotel, the downtown Marriot Courtyard. Maxwell could not keep his hands off Charmin in the hallway. He started to undress her before they had even entered the room. He took her by surprise when he pushed her back against the wall. His kisses were hard as he held her in a tight embrace, and she wrapped her legs around his, elevating herself against his chest. In a swift motion, Maxwell placed Charmin on the hall desk before they both landed on the floor.

With every movement, clothing was being removed. She extended her arms to allow her blouse to go over her head. In the heat of passion, he lowered her bra cups so her breasts fell out over them. His lips and tongue covered her neck and breasts as he found comfort in her body. Charmin's hands wandered over his body, admiring his strength.

They kissed for what seemed like forever. Charmin tore herself from Maxwell's arms and got on all fours in front of him. Maxwell positioned himself directly behind her and lifted her skirt. He pulled down her panties, resting them around her thighs as he got behind her. He drew down his jeans and boxers, freeing his thick, long shaft to fuck her doggy style. He moved with heavy thrusting motions, in and out of her, as they both capitulated in delight.

They lay on the floor, cuddling. Maxwell asked if she wanted to take a bath with him. She thought it was a very romantic notion and, trying to be poised, stood up.

Maxwell followed her into the bathroom while removing articles of clothing. Charmin turned the water nozzle on and adjusted the level so the water would be lukewarm for their bath. Naked, she stepped into the bath and sat down to allow the water level to rise around her. Maxwell enjoyed watching her submerge her body into the water before joining her. They talked for hours in the bath before realizing the coolness of the water was giving them a chill. That evening, they made love several times before going to sleep. His two-day visit was amazing and lusty fun.

Early in the fall, Maxwell attended a construction management trade school in Miami. Charmin was already attending a state university for business management in New York. The distance between them created fantasies but also a deep loneliness. The notion of phone sex allowed them to become very creative, uninhibited, and free. Yet the absence of physical sex created a yearning that was not easily satisfied.

Maxwell started socializing with coworkers and local friends. His appetite for sex started to expand outside of his relationship with Charmin, as did his desire for alcohol and beer.

It wasn't until Charmin moved to Florida, after they had both graduated from college, that their relationship was able to develop and unite their compatibilities into one. Charmin and Maxwell rented a townhouse in Clearwater. Before moving, she was unable to secure a job, so she decided to temp at a real estate office while Maxwell worked as a construction manager for the state of Florida.

Chapter 5

Cohabitating seemed effortless as they settled into a comfortable, monotonous flow. Charmin enjoyed cooking, reading, and keeping their home clean and inviting. Maxwell shared some cleaning responsibilities along with ensuring their home's financial stability. Their lovemaking varied from one experience to the next because Maxwell enjoyed a variety of sexual play.

Early one Saturday morning, Charmin was in the bathroom shaving her legs when Maxwell walked by and noticed her. Charmin had her left leg elevated against the surface of the tub, and her body was arched while she applied long strokes to remove the hair from her leg.

Maxwell stopped and said, "You are so beautiful."

She replied, "Really? What makes me beautiful?"

"I can't stop looking at you, and your body makes my dick hard every time. I'm in love with you," he said.

"That was nice. I love you too, baby, and thank you."

Maxwell stepped into the bathroom, reached out to Charmin, and pulled her into a tight embrace. "When you are done shaving your legs, will you give me a dick massage?"

"I think I can do that," she said.

While Charmin continued to shave her legs, Maxwell searched for the K-Y oil before returning to the bedroom. As much as he loved having his dick sucked, a dick massage was more relaxing for him. He sat on the edge of the bed waiting for Charmin to enter the room. Once she was finished shaving, she walked into the bedroom and removed her bathrobe. Naked, she got on her knees and crawled toward Maxwell.

"Anything I can do for you while I'm down here?" she asked seductively.

"Yes, I would really appreciate a dick massage. Thank you."

Maxwell watched Charmin as she massaged his dick, smothering it in K-Y oil. The way she applied long strokes while gently twisting his testicles was very relaxing to Maxwell.

"Oh, baby, that feels so good. Can you put my dick in your mouth?"

Without words, she opened her mouth while eyeing Maxwell as she engulfed his cock. He pulled her hair away from her face so not to obscure the view of his dick in her mouth. It was very important to Maxwell that Charmin swallow his love juice; after all, it was made for her, he'd say. Maxwell drank pineapple juice daily to ensure his sperm had a sweet taste, which Charmin could validate.

"Thank you. I love the way your hands and mouth feel against my dick," he said.

"I'm glad you enjoyed it. Anything for my man. I love you."

"Ditto, baby."

Charmin enjoyed waking up next to Maxwell every day and especially loved the nights when they stayed up and talked about life. Sex is something our bodies crave, but intimacy happens when one feels comfortable enough to bare his or her soul to someone else without judgment. Charmin and Maxwell would cook breakfast in the nude, which added a level of fun and closeness. Maxwell wasn't much of a cook, but he enjoyed helping and learning new things.

Some of the best feelings and memories Charmin had were during the early stages of their courtship. Their first kiss, for one, and the way Maxwell had touched her for the first time were priceless memories. Time added another layer of priceless events, such as coming home after a long day at the office to be welcomed and loved, that were invaluable to her. Whenever they were together, simple things like setting a table or rinsing the dishes together had significance. Even running errands together created new layers of closeness between them.

Charmin especially enjoyed their sexual moments when Maxwell made the evenings all about her. He would give her a warm bath with drops of accent oil and adorn the bathroom with candles. Sometimes he would use the bath sponge to wash her body while kissing and groping her with both his hands and lips. He would finger-fuck her into an uncontrollable orgasm while sucking her nipples, or he would passionately fuck her while sharing her bath.

Sex with Maxwell was very exciting and satisfying to her. She would do anything he wanted her to because her love was unconditional. Maxwell enjoyed watching Charmin when they went out together. He enjoyed watching her walk as he admired her ass and the way her body moved against her clothes. Although he would not admit it, Maxwell would get jealous when another man looked at Charmin. However, the admiration of others gave him a feeling of pride, knowing he had something they liked. He measured her with his eyes; every curve and line was seen. A look of intent was always on his face because he adored her so much; a feeling of possession overcame him.

He would fantasize about what he wanted to do to her, which showed in his eyes as he watched her. Charmin could always tell when Maxwell wanted sex because he would get agitated and anxious. His patience for things would be shortened and replaced with anxiety. No matter if they were out, or at a restaurant, he would become temperamental and annoyed because he was not getting his way. He had no patience for waiting when he wanted something right then. Maxwell had a very social personality; he enjoyed meeting and talking to people. However, when he was anxious, he would become quiet and unsocial. Charmin knew how to console him so he could relax and rethink his mood.

Sometimes Maxwell had unconventional ways of initiating sex. While attending a conference in California, Maxwell called home. Charmin was making breakfast when the phone rang.

"Hello?" she said.

"Hey, baby, it's me."

"Hi."

He sounded bewildered, "I've been thinking about you all night. Just need to know if you are wearing panties."

"Yes, I am. Why?" she asked, confused.

"I have such a boner thinking about you," he said.

"Would you like me to fly out?" she asked.

"No. I'll be home in two days. Did you sleep in your panties, or did you already shower and are wearing clean ones?" he asked.

"I haven't showered yet. I am still wearing the panties I slept in."

"Nice! What I'd like you to do is remove them and mail your worn panties to me."

There was silence on the line as Charmin tried to process what he had just asked.

"What?" she replied.

"I want you to take off your worn panties, put them in an envelope, and seal it. Then, go to the post office and mail the envelope to me. Okay? I don't want you to send me clean ones. I only want the ones you slept in and are still wearing."

"Wow. Okay. I've never done that before. You'll be home in two days, right? Or I can fly out to see you," she said.

"Sorry, never mind. I just ... never mind. Sorry." He sounded annoyed and disappointed.

"Okay. If it means that much to you," she responded.

"It does. Thank you. I love you," he said.

"Me too."

"Okay. I'd like you to do that now. Call me after you have mailed them. Okay?"

She never knew what to expect from Maxwell, which always made things very interesting. She slipped off her worn panties and placed them on the table in search of an envelope so she could mail them to Maxwell.

She called Maxwell later that day to confirm she had mailed her worn panties for next-day delivery. He was ecstatic and anxious and thanked her for loving him enough to do that.

The panties arrived at Maxwell's hotel room the next day. Maxwell was extremely pleased. He called her and thanked her again. She didn't try to understand why he needed them—just knowing he did was enough for her. Two days later, Maxwell returned from his trip and made passionate love to Charmin.

As they lay in bed that evening, they talked about their relationship and how it had evolved into this beautiful partnership. Besides their sexual attraction and love for each other, they also gave an account to all the miscommunication that happened between them. Charmin believed Maxwell had a fear of commitment because he thought she had betrayed him early in their relationship.

When they were about twenty years old, she had encountered a male friend whom she had known since middle school. He was five years older than her. Nothing ever happened between them, but Maxwell was bothered by their friendship. When a man feels like a woman has played him, resentment settles in, creating coldness around his heart to protect him from further deception. Therefore, Charmin accepted their long courtship as a way for him to regain trust and help resolve his commitment issues.

They agreed that understanding their differences strengthened their relationship. Maxwell vowed not to jump to any conclusions without first addressing the issue.

Although sex was always wonderful between them, Charmin knew he had slept with other women. Before she moved in, he told her about some of the women, but others he did not share. Apparently, men have double standards for women and find justification to support their actions. Maxwell did not like the feeling of being trapped or confined. Instead, he enjoyed the feeling of being free to love openly. He mentioned to Charmin that he wanted to experience a threesome with her. As much as he loved her, the enjoyment of open sex was exciting to him.

Charmin knew that Maxwell didn't want to lose her, and she didn't know how to help him find the level of balance or comfort he needed. Only time would help him decide what he needed and wanted from her. Maxwell's love for Charmin kept him grounded and wanting more out of their relationship.

Charmin knew he was controlling, which caused them to disagree at times. He had a sense of coldness about him when he was bothered by something, as if nothing could change his mind, which annoyed her. Maxwell knew her personality fluctuated from persuasive to submissive. When she was annoyed by something, it showed on her face, as she wore her emotions on her sleeve. Sometimes they talked past each other, intending to listen to each other but failing. Perhaps the saying "Men are from Mars; Women are from Venus" has some merit. Nevertheless, they loved and cared for each other enough to follow their hearts. They wanted to share a life together, which would allow them to build a bridge spanning their differences.

After four years of living together, Maxwell knew he was ready to settle down with the only woman he fantasized about. Time allowed them to learn each other's habits, character, and peculiarities as they matured into adulthood. The foundation of their union was strong. This allowed their relationship to flourish into its next phase.

The morning sun was hot as Charmin walked down the aisle toward Maxwell. He was standing under a beautifully decorated canopy adorned with white calla lilies and assortments of red roses. Her bridesmaids were dressed in satin sage gowns, with the exception of the maid of honor, who wore a satin peach gown. This color combination looked beautiful against all the groomsmen, who wore tailored white tuxedos. The setting was the Tampa beach property of the Don Cesar Hotel.

The scenery was fitting because not only had the couple met in the Tampa area, but they had also experienced their first date and kiss there. When Maxwell had finally proposed six months prior, they were sitting on the balcony of the Beach Suite Resort, which overlooked the gulf.

Maxwell asked if it was okay to order in instead of eating out, which Charmin thought was a good idea, so he called the hotel restaurant and ordered. Because the refrigerator was already stocked with Sam Adams Summer Ale and pink champagne, he poured some bubbly in two glasses as a toast.

Dinner was delicious, and he stared at her, watching every move before saying, "You are so beautiful and I love you. Thank you for the last four and half years. I'm excited just thinking about the future with you. I want to continue to share my life with just you now and forever. I would really like it if you would agree to marry me and make me a happy man. Would you do me the honor?"

"Oh, Maxwell! I love you too, and you are my life, so it's easy to say yes. I will," she responded.

They both smiled as Maxwell reached into his pocket and pulled out a small, turquoise box from Tiffany's wrapped in a white ribbon. Inside was a beautiful one-carat solitaire brilliant-cut diamond in platinum setting, which he slipped on her left ring finger. They embraced with bear hugs and kisses to seal the agreement. Because of their long courtship, it didn't take long for them to decide on a date.

The mood of the ceremony was very intimate yet elegant as one hundred of their closest friends and family members witnessed their matrimonial union. Charmin looked beautiful in her satin white gown and Maxwell looked dapper in his white tuxedo as they exchanged their vows. Just as the minister pronounced them husband and wife, in the distance a dolphin leaped out of the water, which caused their guests to gasp with joy.

They walked down the white satin-lined walker to the reception area to greet their guests before dashing off to take pictures. The DJ continued the couple's tradition of Motown tunes coupled with pop hits. Maxwell and Charmin's first dance was to "Sparkles" by Cameo as Maxwell held her tightly. The reception lasted for four hours, but the memories would linger forever.

Maxwell whisked his new bride to a remote area on the beach and made passionate love to her under the open skies.

"I love you more, if that's even possible. I can't believe we met almost ten years ago and today you are my bride. Thank you for marrying me and making me so happy."

"I'm a lucky woman to have someone as wonderful as you. Thank you for asking me to share your life. I love you."

With her satin white gown rolled up to her waist, exposing her Brazilian-waxed skin, Maxwell drove his thick, hard shaft inside her with deep, hard thrusting motions again. He exploded his love juice inside her well, causing her to orgasm out of control.

That evening in bed, Maxwell and Charmin lay near each other and promised to be open and honest with their needs and desires. The morning light woke them as they prepared to leave the hotel en route to the airport.

Their honeymoon was in Saint Barthelemy. As the fifteen-passenger charter air jet approached the narrow runway, the span of the island loomed vast and mountainous. They felt the warmth of the air as they dismounted and walked down the runway toward the immigration office. They encountered another honeymooning couple who seemed too young to marry, especially compared to Charmin and Maxwell, both in their late twenties. Once cleared by immigration, Maxwell searched for the car rental office.

He had made a reservation while stateside for a jeep for on-call use only, as the villa was centered on an all-inclusive resort. Maxwell handed Charmin a map to help direct him toward the villa.

"I think we just need to head up this road for about three or four miles before making a right turn into the villa."

Reading the map proved effective. After a short period, the resort was in front of them. Maxwell and Charmin entered their rented two-bedroom villa, where they would stay for ten days.

After their long travel day, Charmin wanted to try out the

European shower, which was beautifully designed in warm earth tones. The shower had a walk-in entrance and was equipped to fit more than two people. The model had seven showerheads, three sets on each side, and a wide nozzle overhead that allowed water to just stream over oneself or jet hard against one's body.

Cool water rushed over Charmin's body as Maxwell pressed against her, crushing her breasts against the cold, wet ceramic tiles. His kisses were hard and passionate against the back of her neck before he lowered his face to the dividing line between her cheeks. She reached her hands over her head and up the tiles, as if to climb them, while his face was nestled between her cheeks.

She felt his face forcefully separated her cheeks to find her wet spot with his tongue, while his nose tickled her asshole, giving her a feeling of analingus. A feeling of erotic ecstasy rushed over her while he separated her thighs, and he forced her to arch her back to allow his invasion.

A loud moan of pleasure escaped her lips as she enjoyed his tongue against her clit, wanting him to dart his tongue deeper inside her. As he did just that, his nose continued to give her a tingling feeling of erotic sensation. Aware of what he was doing to her, his tongue moved from her pussy to her asshole, licking and forcing his tongue inside her chocolate shoot. She had given him the same oral pleasure, and now it was her turn. She reached down and started to touch herself to show him how excited she was.

An orgasm unlike any she had ever experienced cascaded over her, causing her to flop against the ceramic tiles like a fish out of water. His dick coupled her out-of-body experience from the rimming simulation. As his hard, thick shaft pinned her against the tiles, thrusting and fucking her, she felt an intense feeling on her breasts, only to realize he was pinching her nipples. As he kissed and sucked her neck with every thrust, she lost footing as the lock between them elevated her like a hook.

Later that evening, she watched Maxwell as he moved around the villa, showing his nakedness as his shaft hung low with pride. Because of their seclusion, dressing was optional in the villa. Maxwell called in an order of fresh crabs and shrimp, which was delivered by a local restaurant. Dressed in bathrobes, they enjoyed a romantic dinner out on the patio overlooking the Caribbean Sea.

The morning light was hot and bright, offering a view of the large, spacious room of the villa. The layout was wonderfully crafted to entice all those who entered to fall in love and lust. As Charmin laid on her stomach facing the open window, the warmth of the air felt like silk against her naked skin as she reflected on her new life as a married woman.

The view was broad and wide, allowing her to see past the master suite into the open foyer, which embodied a Caribbean flair of island colors and wicker chairs. The open room shared earth-toned colors of browns, yellows, and white. Because it was a tropical island, ceiling fans were scattered about the villa. Some of the windows had glass shutters, and others were made of wood, which allowed the air to circulate. The flooring had a marble appearance throughout the main villa, but the bedrooms had wood floors.

Suddenly, she felt a brush of pain against her backside. Unaware of what had caused it, she turned toward Maxwell and said, "What was that?"

He was smiling at her and said, "Good morning, love."

And she said, "Good morning, sweetie. What was that?"

Then Maxwell said, "I'm sorry if that scared you, but your ass seemed so inviting that I just had to spank it." He enjoyed watching how it moved under his hands, he explained. "I'd like to spank you, if that's okay. I'll understand if you don't want me to, but I just find it to be a turn-on."

Her body was relaxed and open to whatever adventure he wanted to explore. She recognized she was with the man she loved and wanted to grow old with, so why not? "Let me take my pill first."

The contraception pack was sitting on the nightstand to remind Charmin in the mornings. She lifted herself from her position and arched her back. When she found herself on all fours, he said in a low tone, "Face me."

She turned toward him to find his hard, thick shaft in her face, so she opened her mouth and took him in. While staring in his eyes, she started to suck and lick. Her tongue went up and down his shaft as her hot, wet mouth swallowed him whole.

While he reached over her and spanked her ass, he stood up on the bed and held her hair in a bunch while he looked down at her sucking his shaft and smiled to himself. He reached over again and spread her cheeks, exposing her to the open air as his finger found her wet opening, and he started finger-fucking her into an orgasm.

Then, with quickness, he took his shaft out of her mouth and said, "I'm not ready to cum; I want to enjoy you some more."

Not sure what that meant, she continued looking at him as he climbed down and walked around to the other side of the bed, stopping in front of her open, exposed, arched ass, which he then started spanking again, each slap giving way to a red handprint. He spanked her ass hard at times, but then asked her to tell him if he should continue or stop.

She said, "Don't stop."

He asked her to face him again so she could take him in her mouth and suck the ready juice out of him because he wanted to juice in her mouth only, not give her a cum facial this time. He told her not to spill any or he would be obliged to spank her again. With her hot wet mouth wrapped around his shaft, she sucked as the stream flowed out.

She tried to swallow it all, but his hot, sticky stream was fast, and the thickness of the cream caused some juice to drip out of the corner of her mouth and trickle down her chin.

He said, "I love watching you with my love juice on your face, but I owe you a spanking."

She swallowed hard and used her tongue to lick any juice that was around her mouth, which he enjoyed watching. They cuddled in bed while his hands tightly cupped her full breasts and she locked her arms around his embrace. They slept until noon in a tight embrace.

Maxwell and Charmin lounged in the large foyer playing chess for the remainder of the day. They relaxed on the lounge chairs and ordered fresh tuna steaks with fries for dinner. Maxwell drank Red Stripe beer while Charmin enjoyed pink champagne. Later that evening, they took advantage of the well-lit infinity pool, which offered a spectacular view of the island and sea, with a little skinny-dipping.

As the sun started to set in the beautiful blue skies, Charmin and Maxwell set off for an early breakfast and to explore what the island had to offer. Eating fresh mangos and pineapple along with mahi-mahi for lunch, they took in a spectacular view from a local restaurant. She was wearing a long, white, sleeveless, flowing dress with no undergarment. A string tied behind her neck held the dress together.

The dress showcased her full breasts, and her perky nipples were exposed as the sun hit the fabric, making it appear sheer. She wore her favorite wedge heels, and he was wearing khaki shorts and white T-shirt. They smiled at each other as they enjoyed their meal. He wanted to take in the sights by jeep, and she wanted to take pictures of the beautiful mountain views against the Caribbean Sea.

The rented jeep had no air conditioning, so they relied on the openness of the jeep and welcomed the warm air that surrounded them as they sent out on their excursion—which included a great deal of sexual misbehaving.

Chapter 6

A couple hours and two rolls of film later, it was Charmin's turn to feel horny. She looked over at Maxwell, admiring his strong facial expression and heavy concentration. Then, she raised both of her legs onto the dashboard, showing her hot-pink polished toes and allowing the wind to bring back the length of her dress, exposing her Brazilian bikini wax.

She then slowly put two fingers in her mouth and sucked them both at the same time. Then she reached between her legs and separated her lips, exposing her clitoris, which she gently rubbed while laying her head back against the headrest. She proceeded to rub her clitoris with her eyes closed until she felt Maxwell's strong hands reaching over to her side, wanting to play with her clitoris too. She let him take over as she opened herself wider to accept his large fingers. He rubbed and fingered her while she bit her lips and moaned with enjoyment. She could feel the sensation spreading across her body with every touch, and she relished the need for more. The sounds of the engine stopping caused her to open her eyes.

Maxwell smiled at her and said, "I love that you love sex."

He leaned over and plowed his face between her thighs; she felt everything from his lips to his tongue to his fingers. She was enjoying the cunnilingus her husband was giving her. Maxwell asked her to stand up and raise her dress, so she stood on the seat and straddled over him.

He leaned forward, holding both of her legs to support her weight, and proceeded to lick and suck her minora. She kept biting her lips in enjoyment. Opening her eyes, she realized she had accomplished her mission: first, finding a spectacular view of the Caribbean Sea, and second, misbehaving. Her orgasm caused her knees to give out as she landed hard on his lap, giggling and laughing as they kissed passionately.

He unfastened the strings behind her neck and rolled down the support of her dress, revealing her full breasts, and then he started to suck and bite her nipples as she held him close, enjoying every moment. He took her hands and led her to the backseat. As she started to climb in, he stopped her and said, "This is good." She was arched sideways with one leg elevated. He stood halfway up and kissed her exposed canal, and then shoved his shaft inside her.

Holding her leg straight up, he fucked her in a scissor-style position with deep, heavy thrusts for about ten minutes. Then, he helped her back to the front seat and asked her to sit on his stiff shaft, which she graciously did. While she moved her body with deep muscle movements and grinding motions, she milked his cum out as he sucked on her breasts. She flexed her kegel muscles to tighten her grip around his shaft and, with her left hand, cupped his balls. At the same time, she pinched at his nipples, hard at times, with her right hand.

They were unaware that tourists were nearby, so they continued to fuck until his semen launched inside her. His body was relaxed as the semen flowed out of him and into her. Being so wet, she could not tell what was his and what was hers. The thought that he was inside of her was exhilarating.

As Charmin lifted her legs to dismount Maxwell, she noticed

a creamy white liquid streaming out of her and down her legs. She reached for her white dress, settled on the jeep floor, and discretely wiped off the excess cum, hoping not to stain her dress. Clothed, they continued their excursion, and Charmin closed her eyes to take in the warm sun and reflect on her erotic honeymoon.

The couple decided to stop at Saint Jean beach and walk along the white, sandy shoreline. Neither of them had packed bathing suits because the privacy around the villa allowed them to swim nude all the time. However, they acknowledged that they were not on an all-exclusive beach; it was a public beach, so tact was in order.

Maxwell decided to rent a large umbrella and double lounge chair to lie on, take in the view, and nap. When Charmin napped, Maxwell decided to venture off to see what possibilities lay ahead.

Unaware of the time lapse, Charmin felt her lips being kissed, and she awoke. As she opened her eyes, a greenish-blue stone-like object was dangling in her face. Maxwell had bought her a beautiful earring and necklace set, which had been handmade by a native who owned a jewelry shop on the island.

Charmin took off her gold studs and replaced them with her new earrings and necklace. Seeing her wear the jewelry gave Maxwell a feeling of accomplishment and pride. He lay near her on the chair, and she placed her head on his chest while they talked about their dreams and fantasies. The loud roaring sound of a plane overhead reminded Charmin of their youthful encounter at Orlando International Airport.

Maxwell had been seeing Charmin off after they'd enjoyed spring break together. Her flight was a red-eye, and the airport seemed deserted. She needed to wash her hands before boarding the plane, so she told Maxwell she'd be right back. However, as she headed to the ladies' room, she noticed that Maxwell had followed her. He grabbed ahold of her tightly and said, "I want to fuck you—here, in the airport bathroom."

Charmin turned on the water faucet to wash her hands while glaring at him in the mirror. Maxwell lifted up her miniskirt, exposing her white panties. She watched him in the mirror as he placed his hand inside her panties, touching her that way for the first time. She was so into him that nothing mattered. He unzipped his pants and exposed his long, thick shaft while she pulled down her panties and raised her leg onto the sink top. Maxwell held her for support. She could see his thick shaft spreading her open and disappearing inside of her.

Reaching for the cold mirror, Charmin started feeling heat run through her. As Maxwell's hips started to thrust back and forth, the couple stared at each other in the mirror. Maxwell said, "Just before I start to juice, I want you to take it in your mouth." She agreed and got on her knees. But as she opened her mouth, his hot sticky load ejected out onto her face.

She tried to close her eyes, but his stream was strong. Maxwell gasped to say, "I'm sorry," but he realized he liked having his juice on her face. The thickness of his white cum sliding down her nose and chin and onto her peach top was the beginning of her cum facials with him.

Returning to the villa from their excursion called for a refreshing swim in the pool, which was done in the nude because of their seclusion. Charmin's full breasts moved in slow motion underwater as she paddled her legs in and out, every part of her body completely exposed. His silhouette was that of leanness with a large, heavy penis dancing up and down in the water. They swam, dived, and lounged in the pool, turning prune-like. Just before sunset, they dressed and headed out for dinner and a little dancing.

At the local bar, filled with beautiful people having fun, they danced and moved to the island sounds. Charmin was sipping on pink champagne and Maxwell was downing Red Stripe. Charmin searched through the crowd to see whom they could pair up with as a social outing for the evening. Meanwhile, Maxwell was staring at a tall, double-D local wearing a short, deep-V, light yellow dress that accentuated her large breasts

Charmin continued to watch her husband with interest. At first, she was concerned—they had crazy sex all the time, so why the need to search out? However, she remembered that she wanted to try understanding his need for diversity and his preference for variety. It would take her many years of trial and error to understand that side of him.

Charmin walked toward Maxwell and smiled, saying, "See anything you like?"

He smiled back. "Maybe!"

Charmin reached under her short turquoise dress and proceeded to remove her thong with one hand while resting the other on his shoulder. She was able to remove it and handed her red thong to him and said, "Let me know what you want to do!"

The look of surprise and approval on his face told her they would have company—not only at dinner, but also in bed.

As she walked back to the bar stool to continue watching Maxwell she noticed a few admirers watching her while she watched him. She wondered what the events of the night would mean for them. Did this mean they were swingers, or just on their honeymoon having out-of-the-box sex? What was her role—watch while he caressed and fucked her or the two of them, allowing him to have his way with them? Unsure, she decided to let the evening present itself. Suddenly, she noticed he was no longer standing where she had last seen him. So she searched the room and found him near the native, talking.

Charmin watched while he danced with the native. Then he reached his hand out, asking Charmin to join them, and she did. She stood behind and the native in front, sandwiching him in with heavy grinding and body rubbing. Charmin was becoming surprisingly aroused. While they danced, Maxwell reached back and caressed her thighs.

Then, from out of nowhere, someone appeared behind Charmin, rubbing and breathing heavily, and started to caress her neck. Before she could turn, Maxwell stopped dancing and turned toward Charmin with a look of rage, and suddenly, the presence was no longer behind her. She wondered why it was okay for him to dance with someone else but not for her. They needed to talk about that situation, so she tabled the thought for a later time.

The bar was filled with natives, along with a few tourists; some were married or coupled, yet many seemed single. She wondered what had attracted him to this particular native, as many women seem dressed for sexual encounters. Why her?

As they stopped dancing, Maxwell whispered in Charmin's ear, "I want her to suck my dick. Is that okay?"

Charmin was not surprised. She only wondered if she could handle it. "Okay," she said. Maxwell held Charmin's hands and led her to a hallway near the bathroom, where the large-breasted native was waiting. He kissed Charmin with an open mouth and pinched her nipples at the same time to arouse her. He then turned to the native and cupped her large breasts in his hands, while also pinching her nipples. Her facial expression revealed that she was very turned on.

He exposed one of the native's large breasts, which had a hook-like shape to it, the nipple acting as the point. His tongue licked her nipple as he stared at her. She told him to stop teasing her and just fuck her. Maxwell stopped, looked at Charmin, and turned back to her to say, "I only want you to suck my dick." Disappointed, the native fell to her knees and unzipped his pants to free his dick and then started to suck and lick his shaft with hunger.

Charmin watched her man being turned on by another woman, and she knew she was not the only one watching this sexual act. She didn't care, since she was not a native of the island, only a visitor. The native woman took Maxwell's heavy juice flow in stride and swallowed hard and fast, so as not to stain her dress, an act to be impressed by. Maxwell helped the native up and zipped his pants as he kissed her on her cheeks and whispered, "Nice!"

As they returned to the open bar area, some folks were well aware of what had happened, while others seemed unmoved. Charmin and Maxwell invited the native, who introduced herself as Katlyn, for drinks at their barstool. Katlyn went on to explain her behavior, saying she had never done that before; she had just broken up with her boyfriend and felt lonely.

Maxwell commented, "No need to explain; we are not judging you. I personally enjoyed your blow job."

Charmin didn't say much; she only wondered what Maxwell wanted to do next with this native. Katlyn was twenty-six years old and full of life and vitality. She was also educated and held a good job—nothing odd about her. The conversation seemed to flow, and she was very interesting. A newfound friend and playmate, perhaps?

Charmin and Maxwell walked back to the jeep hours later. She needed to present her thoughts, so she asked him, "Didn't you want to have a ménage-à-trois with that native? Yet you could not allow another man to touch me?"

In response, he said, "I love you and don't want another man to enjoy you as I do. I know it doesn't seem fair, but with men, it's really just sex. With women, there are emotions that can be difficult to separate."

Charmin exclaimed, "I have no interest in fucking another man, but I wanted to understand your view, which I now do. Your needs are greater than mine is what I understood."

An educated woman, she knew that battle would not be won here and now, or maybe ever, so she dropped the issue for the moment.

On their ten-minute drive back to the villa, she decided to unzip his pants and give him a hand job. Pulling on his shaft and gently squeezing his balls, she could feel him getting harder as he drove. He started to gasp and moan and said, "Don't make me cum yet. I want to feel your tight grip around my shaft."

As they entered the villa, she pulled her dress up over her head because he already had her thong. She was naked and walked toward the infinity pool. The light from the moon gave her a sexy silhouette. Her breasts were full and round, and her nipples protruded outward. The roundness of her full ass and waxed pussy gave her an inviting appeal.

She walked into the second bedroom, removed her vibrator from her luggage, and returned to the pool area. She relaxed on the plush patio lounge chair and spread her legs. She looked at Maxwell, who was still standing at the doorway, pending an invite. She took her vibrator into her mouth and sucked and licked as if it were him. Then she traced the vibrator down past her stomach to where her thighs separated and proceeded to masturbate.

She laid the vibrator near the opening of her lips, and then raised her right leg over her head and proceeded to let the vibrator in farther as he watched. Maxwell began to disrobe and walk toward her with excitement. He kissed her hand and took the vibrator away. He unfolded her other leg and extended them both over her head in a spread-eagle position.

He applied pressure to her thighs, forcing her lower back and ass to lift from the lounge chair and pinning her knees against her ears. He stood over her and started to examine her ass with his tongue then a finger before he spread her labia. He exposed her wet canal and gently rubbed against her pink clitoris, causing Charmin to moan. She held both of her legs to allow him full access. Maxwell needed to find a way to stand taller so he could straddle her.

He reached for the metal table nearest to him and pushed it against the lounge chair. He stood with one leg on the table and the other over Charmin, flat on the lounge chair. Trying to keep his balance, he directed his long shaft into Charmin's very open canal and started fucking her with vigor in a squat position, hovering over her body. From her angle, she witnessed every long thrust in and out of her.

Then he took the vibrator and placed it on her clitoris while he thrust deep inside of her. With the vibrator on her clitoris as he fucked her, he was driving her wild, fucking deeper and harder. She cried out with ecstasy from both the orgasm and the need to stretch her legs.

He removed his shaft from inside her and helped her to erect herself, only for him to turn her around and continue in his favorite position of improved doggy style. She arched her back. With the vibrator still in his hand, he rested the vibrator on her asshole. The tingling was incredible. Then he ran off into the second bedroom, leaving her in an inviting position, returning quickly with lube he said, "I'd like to put the vibrator in your asshole while I stick my dick in your pussy."

She thought, "This is a new experience. I've never done that before."

After he poured lubricant in and around her asshole and some on the vibrator, he gently started to put the vibrator in her. Instantly, she felt weird pressure and some discomfort, and he stopped to allow her anal contour to reshape around the vibrator before gently continuing to put the vibrator farther inside her. The vibrator was about 4.5 centimeters wide with a soft gel texture.

The vibrator had been given to her as a wedding gift, and now it was turning into her new butt plug. Once it was inside of her, she felt okay. The pressure subsided and it gave her a comfortable feeling. Realizing she had taken the vibrator in excited him that much more, so he spanked her ass and she released a natural moan, which he enjoyed hearing. He continued to spank her ass before he was ready to put his thick long shaft inside her canal, providing her with the experience of double penetration.

His improved doggy-style position was with one leg on the lounge chair and the other planted on the ground, which gave him good traction for hard, deep penetration. He continued to spank her ass while the vibrator trembled inside her asshole. He reached for her hair and pulled it toward him while he continued to fuck her with passion.

The level of orgasm she kept experiencing was that of intense, out-of-body ecstasy. They fucked for what seemed like hours, as the sweat rolled off her breasts. She could feel the sweat on his legs as she held them from time to time for support. As he exploded, his shaft came out, which caused juice to launch over her head. The remainder of his love potion landed on her back and on the vibrator.

She felt the heavy cream roll down the crack of her ass and just past her canal onto the towel lying on the lounge chair. She reached back to remove the vibrator and brushed her hands against thick levels of cum on her butt cheeks. Maxwell stood, still trying to regain his balance from such an ejaculation because he was riddled with fatigue and completeness. He finally mustered the strength to say, "We fucked like porn stars!"

He reached under her, took the towel, and started to wipe all the excess juice off her back and butt cheeks. She tried to help but was too lightheaded.

Later, as she toweled herself off after a warm shower, he went into a light coma of fatigue. She laid her body near his, and they spooned for the remainder of the night.

Chapter 7

Charmin decided to get up early and take the jeep to the local market for breakfast. As she waited in line to purchase her groceries, Charmin noticed a woman who seemed familiar. It was Katlyn.

Charmin walked toward her and said, "Good morning. Remember me?" Katlyn looked surprised but glad to see her again. "I've just picked up a few things for breakfast. I have fresh bread, eggs, cheese, bacon, strawberries, mangos, and fresh guava juice. Why don't you join us for breakfast, if you haven't already eaten?"

Katlyn smiled and said, "No, I haven't eaten yet. I was just getting a few things myself. I'd like to join you if you are sure it's okay."

"Of course it's fine."

Charmin purchased her groceries, and they walked out together. Katlyn was driving a moped, so she followed Charmin to the villa. Charmin knew that after their wild night they needed nourishment to stay strong and fit; Katlyn was just an added surprise that Maxwell would enjoy.

On her drive back, Charmin relished in the memories of their first four days of vacation and was saddened at the thought of their honeymoon ending in six days. This meant going back to the reality of work and home life responsibility. She decided to continue at her pace of being carefree and open to new adventures, no matter what they were—as long as she and Maxwell did them together, she trusted him and felt safe.

Katlyn helped Charmin with the groceries as they walked into the villa together. Charmin mentioned that Maxwell may still be sleeping and that clothes were usually not worn between them, so she shouldn't be surprised if he walked into the kitchen naked. Katlyn didn't seem to mind.

The aroma of bacon and of eggs, whisked into an omelet sprinkled with salt and pepper for taste, filled the air. The bread smelled oven fresh, and as Charmin sliced it, the scent grew stronger. She rummaged through the cabinets in search of plates, silverware, and regular glasses (not the champagne ones she has been using steadily). Everything always seemed so orderly because of the housecleaners who cared for the villa and whom she had only seen once.

Before she could leave the kitchen to wake Maxwell, he walked in, naked and smiling and said, "Hey, beautiful. What's cooking?" He was unaware that Katlyn was in the pantry. Charmin stared at him and started to undress. This happened easily because she was braless in a light pink top with a matching tricolor miniskirt and no underwear.

Then Charmin said, "Have a seat, sweetie, and I'll show you."

He took a seat and placed the cloth napkin over his lap, covering his strong shaft. A look of surprise crossed Maxwell's face as he watched Katlyn coming from the pantry.

"Good morning," Katlyn said. "I guess I should undress too. It's only polite."

Katlyn proceeded to remove her sundress, revealing her large breasts and black thong, which she also slipped off. They proceeded to serve Maxwell, and he enjoyed being catered to. Breakfast was very tasty, but dessert was about to follow as Charmin led Katlyn into the large foyer overlooking the pool.

Charmin asked, "Would you still like to fuck my husband?"

Katlyn said, "If that's okay."

"Yes, it is," Charmin replied.

"First, why don't we give him something to enjoy watching?"

"What do you mean?"

"Well, he enjoys women, and we are both women," Katlyn whispered.

A look of surprise swept over Charmin's face because the thought of letting a woman touch her had never been an option or interest.

"I love men—in particular my husband because he has a shaft that I enjoy," Charmin whispered back.

"I'm really sorry if I have offended you," Katlyn said.

Charmin clearly was but played it off like everything was fine. Katlyn moved to the center of the foyer and started to play with her breasts as she eyed Maxwell with an inviting smile.

Charmin turned to Maxwell and said, "This wasn't planned, but you have two women who want you. What are you going to do about it?"

Maxwell walked toward Charmin, embraced her tightly, and said, "I love you, babe, but my plan is to fuck you only." He walked over to Katlyn, firmly grabbed her breasts, smiled, and said, "It's really nice to see you again—this time with no clothes. You are a beautiful woman, but I love fucking my wife. However, I did enjoy your blow job, if you don't mind giving me another one of those."

Without hesitating, she got on her knees and started to suck on Maxwell's shaft while firmly cupping his balls. Charmin joined in on the fun. She started on the opposite side and spread his ass cheeks to give him analingus, using her finger to tickle his hole. Maxwell loved it.

He asked Katlyn to stop sucking his shaft because he wanted to fuck Charmin. Reaching behind him, he pulled her up and asked Charmin to assume the position. The only position that did not require thought was his favorite position: doggy style. She positioned herself on all fours on the lounge chair.

However, Maxwell wanted to try something else and asked her to place a towel on the floor instead, so she did. Charmin's canal was arched and ready for entry. Maxwell positioned himself behind her, standing up with his knees slightly bent. He asked her to arch her ass higher, and she did, allowing Maxwell to penetrate her at an angle.

The rhythm was hard, fast, and animal-like. His hands were holding onto her shoulders tightly as he thrust hard like a tiger. Katlyn decided to suck on his balls while he was fucking Charmin. Her tongue and mouth tried to keep up with his fast rhythm of doggy style that slammed hard against Charmin's love hole. Maxwell took his shaft out of Charmin, intending to blow his load against her back, only to be intercepted by Katlyn, who took his shaft in her mouth and swallowed his hot, sticky load.

Maxwell yelled out, "I'm a lucky guy to have a wife who would do something like that for me! I do love sex, but babe, I love fucking you."

That was all Charmin needed to know and hear because it gave her comfort and eased her mind, knowing that Maxwell would not need to fool around behind her back and that he respected her enough to tell her when and if that desire presented itself.

The rest of the day was low-key, filled with jokes and interesting tales about each other, along with eating grilled cheese sandwiches, lounging around, reading, and searching the Internet for stateside current events. Just before midnight, Katlyn left. They planned to get together again before leaving the island. Charmin decided to cap off Maxwell's evening with a deep-throat blow job, which caused him to moan as he ejected love juice down her throat. She swallowed all of it.

The early morning presented the idea of jet-skiing and possible deep-sea diving. Charmin really didn't see herself deep-sea diving, but she knew she would enjoy watching Maxwell suited up and photographing underwater sea life. They set off to rent jet skis and wet suits to tackle the unknown current of the water, which proved very rough at times and surprisingly cold the farther out they went, between four and six miles from the shoreline. They raced at times and just enjoyed the magnificent view of the island.

Maxwell inquired about the deep-sea diving, about nine miles from shore, which guaranteed beautiful sea life. The large vessel sailed them out to the open sea, where they encountered heavy currents that at times got very rocky before settling into calm waters. Charmin wore a navy blue minidress with sexy sandals that wrapped around her ankles as she lounged at the edge of the large vessel watching Maxwell. He seemed ready and capable even though he'd never gone deep-sea diving before. Three hours of learning how to breathe underwater was coupled with one hour of learning how to allow water to enter the wet suit for gravity. Maxwell was having a grand time. Upon returning to shore, Maxwell recounted his experience as fantastic.

The open sea had given both of them a strong appetite. Instead of returning to the villa and changing for dinner, they decided to wear what they had, which meant a more casual restaurant then what they had experienced since arriving on the island.

After dinner, the drive seemed longer than usual; because the day had been filled with water activities, the open, hot air was causing fatigue to settle in for both of them. A hot shower to rinse off the salt water and add coolness to their bodies capped off the night. Sleep seemed to wash over them once their heads hit the pillows, still locked in each other's arms.

During the night, Maxwell awoke to get some ice and cold water to drink. Charmin also woke up and joined him in the kitchen. They shared a glass of ice water while smiling at each other. She then took some ice into her mouth and started to kiss Maxwell, enticing him with her wet lips and mouth.

She started to kiss his neck and chest, stopping at his nipples, which she started biting and sucking with her cold tongue. He seemed to enjoy it, so she reached down and cupped his balls with her hands, gently squeezing them while she licked his nipples. She lowered herself while he reached for something to support his arched leg. She took his shaft into her mouth and sucked it, causing it to harden.

The ice in her mouth created a heavy wetness around his shaft that made his hips move in a fucking motion against her mouth. She continued to suck his shaft and balls, first one at a time, and then both at the same time. During the act of fellatio, cold saliva started to stream from the corner of her mouth, wetness trickling down her chin onto her breasts before settling on the floor. He loved seeing that.

She used her fingers to tickle his asshole before using her tongue, which he enjoyed that much more. He lifted her up and moved toward the kitchen table, where he stretched her arms across the table as she leaned forward, spreading her legs and arching her back.

Maxwell positioned himself directly behind her, enjoying the view of her well-exposed ass. He stuck two of his fingers inside of her wet beaver. As he finger-fucked her, he started spanking her ass. He shoved his hard shaft inside her tight, wet hole, fucking her so hard, the table moved a few times. She moaned with enjoyment as he continued to spank her ass until he exploded his hot load inside of her.

Returning to bed, Maxwell said, "My dick is so happy. I can't believe how much fun we are having together. Thank you for liking sex enough to try different things with me. I love you, babe."

Charmin leaned into Maxwell to rest her head on his chest before going back to sleep.

The sky was dark and gray. Heavy clouds brought the anticipation of a storm of sorts. Watching the rage of the sea from the backyard of the villa, they knew it would be an indoor activity day. Maxwell decided to play catch-up via e-mail before connectivity was lost, and Charmin decided to shave her underarms, legs, and pubic area. Maxwell normally enjoyed watching this, but he seemed to be engrossed in his e-mails.

She searched through her vanity case for the shaving cream and a razor and found both. She started for the bathroom but caught a glimpse of her silhouette in the full mirror, causing her to stop and admire herself. Charmin brushed her fingers through her hair before pinning it up, and touched her breasts and nipples quietly, smiling at all the attention and action they'd seen. As she continued to look at herself, she realized her pussy was getting a physical workout seemingly every day.

She touched her lips, tracing their contours. In the faint distance, she could her Maxwell on his cell phone conversing with a colleague, which reminded her of her task, so she headed toward the bathroom. She stepped into the shower stall and creamed her underarm. She started to remove her underarm hair using a daisy razor, one stroke at a time, and then rinsed off before proceeding to cream her legs, which she had elevated on top of the built-in ceramic bench.

She glided up and down her legs, each stoke removing unwanted hair. Maxwell entered the bathroom in search of her, only to stop and admire the view of her shaving. Charmin enjoyed him watching her as she continued to shave her legs with long strokes, causing her to reach forward and arch her back, giving him a side view of her ass.

Maxwell said, "I love when you do that!"

Charmin smiled in delight. She rinsed off her legs, leaving a smooth surface. Then she sat on the cold, wet ceramic bench and spread her legs wide, which caused her lips to part and exposed her subtle clitoris. Each lip was surrounded by new hair growth that tickled her at times. She reached for the cream but was intercepted by Maxwell who wanted to cream and shave off her pubic hair.

He creamed his hands and then applied the cold cream over her pubic area. He knelt on the cold wet ceramic floor and elevated her legs onto his shoulders, allowing for full access. Gently, he moved the razor against her skin as he removed her pubic hair. Charmin stared at him in wonderment as he shaved her. Each stroke gave way to an erotic feeling.

Nearing her lips, he handed her the razor, unable to continue for fear of hurting her. Instead, he watched as Charmin spread her lips and closely shaved each lip. Just as she finished, Charmin looked at Maxwell and said, "It's your turn." He stood erect and firm while she creamed the area surrounding his long, hung shaft and proceeded to shave him with gentle strokes. As she held his shaft in her hand, she elevated it so she could shave the hairs on his balls. Now they were both clean-shaven and smooth again.

Charmin, already in a kneeling position, took his thick shaft in her mouth and started to suck on his dick while cupping his balls. She exchanged her mouth for her hands and started to stroke his shaft. With her hands moving up and down, taking in his balls one at a time then both at the same time, she traced the tip of his balls with her tongue.

Repositioning herself, she nestled her face between his thighs and under his balls. While in a semi-squat position, she started to vigorously stroke his shaft. She used her free hand to spread his cheeks so she could entice his honey pot with her finger. While she vigorously stroked, pre-cum started to settle around her grip as he reached under himself to pull her up so as not to blow his load too soon. He positioned her on the wet bench and knelt in front of Charmin's groin. He darted his tongue in between her lips and sucked and licked her minora, teasing her until she experienced an orgasm.

An interesting sound similar to a doorbell chimed throughout the villa. Though neither was dressed, Maxwell headed for the door with a towel around his waist, and Charmin also held a towel around her body. As he opened the door, a gust of wind and rain entered before he could see who it was.

"Hello. I hope I'm not intruding," said the stranger.

"No, not at all. Hello, Katlyn," Maxwell said.

"I was wondering if you wouldn't mind helping me. Rain is coming into my house through the windows; I can't stop it. Do you mind?"

Maxwell invited her in. She was completely wet, her hair stuck to her face and her yellow T-shirt soaked, revealing her voluptuous breasts and hard nipples through her sheer bra. She wore white shorts revealing her panty outline and cute flip-flops.

Maxwell called out to Charmin as she entered the foyer. A look of surprise and concern rushed over her. "What's wrong?" she asked.

"I need help. Too much water is coming inside my house," Katlyn said.

Maxwell hurried off to dress and Charmin did the same. "Give us a minute," Maxwell said.

Katlyn only had a moped, so Maxwell asked her to leave it and to get in the jeep. En route to Katlyn's home, the mood of what to expect was circling both their minds. Was this some type of game to fuck Maxwell, or was it sincere?

Chapter 8

Nestled low behind several tall palm trees was Katlyn's house, a quaint-looking home surrounded by a beautiful view and coconut trees.

As they walked through the front door, they had a view of the entire house. They could hear the wind whistling throughout it. Maxwell marched toward the kitchen window and saw water streaming in and wet towels. He indicated that the seal around the window was worn and needed to be replaced.

"Do you have a tool box?"

"Yes."

Katlyn left the room and returned with a large metal box given to her by her ex-boyfriend, whose pictures still decorated the house. Maxwell searched through the box and found a rubber-like weather strip. As he opened the window, water poured in. He worked quickly to remove and replace the strip, getting soaked in the process.

Katlyn led Charmin into her bedroom in search of towels. As Charmin entered her chambers, she saw that there were bottles of body oils, lubricant, tickle whips, candles, and different size dildos and butt plugs. Katlyn once again was not moved by the intrusion. They returned to the kitchen with a handful of towels to help dry Maxwell off and help absorb all the water around the kitchen sink and floor.

Katlyn jested to Maxwell and Charmin, "It's okay if you want to take off your clothes. We can spread them out to help dry faster— besides, I owe you a blow job as payment."

Maxwell smiled at Charmin and started to undress, as did Charmin and Katlyn. Maxwell removed his T-shirt and shorts, and Charmin removed her black-and-white minidress. Neither of them wore underwear, so they were naked in no time.

"Can I offer either of you a drink?" Katlyn moved toward the refrigerator.

"No, thanks. We're good," Maxwell said.

"Then maybe I can offer you a more comfortable setting. Follow me," Katlyn motioned forward and removed her wet clothing. Charmin knew where she was headed and that Maxwell would enjoy that setting.

"Nice!" exclaimed Maxwell. "Wow, is this all yours?"

"Yes, my boyfriend and I enjoyed sex a great deal!"

"Cool." Maxwell walked toward the bed and sat down as he examined the room for all that it had to offer. "How about a dick massage? This oil is guaranteed to satisfy."

Katlyn walked over to her dresser and grabbed a tall bottle of heated lubricant oil with a hint of chocolate flavor. She asked Maxwell to lay back and relax as she started to pour the oil over his shaft. As one hand rubbed the oil around his shaft and balls, the other held the bottle.

Charmin was full of surprises. She climbed on the bed and positioned herself over Maxwell's face in a sixty-nine position. She and Katlyn could share the licks and sucks of Maxwell's chocolate-flavored shaft while she got her pussy licked and fingered by him. Intense licking and sucking caused both Katlyn and Charmin to come dangerously close to each other's lips and tongues. This alarmed Charmin, and she retracted and allowed Katlyn more space.

Katlyn reached for one of her dildos and decided to squat on an eight-inch toy on the floor in front of Maxwell's shaft while they continued to share licks and sucks. It seemed everyone was being pleasured at the same time.

Charmin lifted her wet pussy from Maxwell's face, only to turn and face him. She kissed his wet lips and spanked him with her voluptuous D-sized breasts. "Bad boy," she said. While tit-slapping Maxwell, Charmin did not realize she had arched her ass, which was now exposed and facing Katlyn.

"You have a beautiful round ass good for fucking," Katlyn said.

Charmin acknowledged the compliment and said, "Thank you. Yours isn't so bad, either."

"Thanks," she said.

"I have butt plugs. Would you like to use one?"

Maxwell's voice carried, "Nice!"

"Do you have condoms? I can't use your butt plug without a condom," Charmin said.

"I'm sure I do," Katlyn said. "Let me look around."

Maxwell decided to get off the bed while Charmin positioned herself on all fours with her ass facing Maxwell, awaiting a butt plug. Maxwell playfully spanked her ass hard.

"My shaft can't wait," he said as he shoved his dick inside her very wet canal and started to fuck her with a slow rhythm.

Katlyn approached with the butt plug and proceeded to put the condom on it in front of Maxwell, further enticing him. Then she looked at Maxwell with a smile. "Let me," she said as she poured lubricate on Charmin's asshole and gently pushed the butt plug in, before handing it off to Maxwell. Charmin was experiencing heavy moans and biting her lips while embracing his rhythm.

Katlyn mounted the bed and straddled Charmin's back. Facing Maxwell, she held an eight-inch dildo in her hands, which she proceeded to put in her mouth while licking and playfully sucking before tracing it down her stomach and applying in inside her wet canal, which now rested on Charmin's back.

Katlyn watched as Maxwell fucked Charmin with both his shaft and the butt plug. With her free hand, she started playing with her breasts, pinching her nipples. Then she gripped her large breasts, pointing them toward her face so she could lick her breasts and nipples. While she eyed Maxwell, her extended tongue brushed against her own nipples, and then Maxwell leaned forward and extended his tongue, allowing them to jointly lick and suck on her nipples.

"Having fun?" Charmin asked.

"Yep! I sure am," he said.

The rush of his semen was similar to a rush of lava near the brink of volcanic eruption. He pulled his shaft out of Charmin and pointed it toward Katlyn. The ejaculation of hot-spurring cream launched out onto Katlyn's breasts and landed on Charmin's ass. Maxwell took a deep breath while enjoying the view of his juice on a pair of large breasts dripping down onto a beautiful ass. Katlyn climaxed shortly after, and Charmin experienced multiple orgasms. Trying to recover from their fuck fest, they lay in bed together and enjoyed the warmth of each other's bodies.

The noise of the heavy rain woke them several hours later. Charmin turned to Maxwell and asked, "Ready, sweetie?" to which he replied, "I am." Their clothes were semidry because of the dampness from the rain, but they didn't seem to mind as Charmin and Maxwell both embraced Katlyn good-bye.

"Thank you for this experience. We'll be leaving the island the day after next. Thank you, sweetie," Charmin said.

Maxwell turned toward Katlyn, kissed her on the cheek, and said, "I'll always remember you and those juicy tits."

Katlyn mentioned a friend would drop by to collect her moped, if that was okay.

"No problem," Maxwell said.

On the drive back to the villa, Maxwell said, "I can't believe I'm married to you. We should have been fucking like this all along." He extended his fingers to his nose and smelled them. "I love the way you smell, babe," Maxwell said. Charmin knew that in her youth, she was too refined to be this carefree and open, and only time had allowed her to relax her ways.

On their short drive back to the villa, Charmin reminded Maxwell that he too was not as open and carefree in his youth. Maxwell replied, "When was I ever afraid to be open about sex?"

"Really? Don't you remember when your mom was visiting? She wanted to see Washington, DC, and all its charm? You forgot you give her a key, and she walked in while you were fucking the curls out of my hair." Laughter rang out in the jeep.

"Oh, okay. She was mad at me for days."

"Okay, I'll accept that one." More laughter consumed the couple.

Once in the villa, Charmin noticed a brochure on the wicker table while Maxwell was taking a swim in the pool. The brochure offered massages, including exotic oil massages, which she was sure would be okay with him. She called to inquire and liked the idea that a licensed masseuse would come to the villa. Glancing at Maxwell, she decided to keep it a surprise to top off their honeymoon. She requested one male and one female masseuse to add balance between them. She scheduled the appointment for ten in the morning, with four hours of deep tissue and exotic oil massages.

The morning light brought a bittersweet feeling, knowing that in twenty-four hours they would be leaving the island. Yet the anticipation of a well-needed massage would help soften that reality. At eight in the morning, Charmin woke and rinsed off in the shower while Maxwell was still sleeping. As she finished off, Maxwell was just getting up, wondering why she was up so early.

Charmin took the opportunity to share the surprise of their pending massages, which Maxwell took in stride, agreeing that it was a great idea to cap off their vacation. At nine forty-five the chiming sound rang again throughout the villa, and Charmin hurried toward the door, knowing the masseuses had arrived. The door opened, and there stood a tall, well-built gentleman and a very full-size, tall woman, both wearing casual attire of white T-shirts and matching shorts.

"Hello, welcome. Please come in."

"Hello. Thank you."

"My name is Hank."

"And I am Wilma."

"We are here to give you and your spouse an oil massage, along with deep tissue concentration. I'd like to set up outside near the pool, if that's okay," Hank said.

"That's fine. Please follow me," Charmin said. "Oh, sorry, I'm Charmin and my husband is Maxwell."

Hank was wheeling two large cots, and Wilma had luggage-like bags.

"If it's okay, we'd like you and your husband to change out of your clothes. Here are two robes to wear."

Maxwell was on his cell phone confirming the flight reservation. He entered as Wilma handed Charmin the robes.

"Hello. I'm Maxwell."

"Hello, sir. I'm Hank, and here is Wilma. Wilma will be giving you your deep tissue massage, and I will be doing the same for your wife, along with a requested oil massage, if that is still okay."

"Yes, that sounds great!"

Charmin and Maxwell both disrobed in the master suite and returned to the poolside. The cots were set up with white sheets and rolled pillows. Charmin disrobed, exposing her nakedness, before mounting her cot.

"I'm not shy. No worries. Okay."

"Very well, miss," Hank said. "Before we begin, I would like to offer scents to complete the setting."

"Okay, what do you have?"

"Well, we have mint, jasmine, citrus, or coconut."

"I'll try the coconut scent," she said.

Hank asked her to roll over on her stomach and place her face between the cushion pillows. As she motioned over, she noticed Maxwell was selecting his scent before glancing over to her and lying on his stomach.

The massage was very relaxing, causing a feeling of intimacy to sweep over Charmin. Hank oiled her body and applied pressure against her buttocks and hips before his hands moved all over her thighs. Then he lifted her legs and massaged her inner thighs. At this point, her body was exposed to Hank. Maxwell was receiving a well-deserved back rub as Wilma extended his arms over his head and massaged them with a firm grip.

Maxwell seemed to enjoy his massage as he turned over, exposing his shaft, before Wilma placed a towel over him. He smiled.

Charmin was in and out of sleep, and her mind started to wander. She started focusing on a house party where she and Maxwell had argued over nothing, just to rekindle their attraction to one another only a moment later. The party was held in a friend's basement, and between twenty-five and thirty young adults were present. She decided to sit at the far end of the room. While everyone around her was either conversing or dancing, she was reflecting on their argument.

Maxwell had entered the basement and started searching for her. When he found her, he walked toward her to ask her to dance, which she did reluctantly, and their bodies jellied together as they moved as one. Passion ran through her as their embrace tightened to a slow dance. They shared the heat and passion between themselves. She laid her head against his chest, and he held her in a tight embrace. They danced for what seemed like an hour before realizing sweat was rolling off their faces and body.

Maxwell had suggested moving upstairs to cool off, but he needed to make a stop at the bathroom, so Charmin waited for him. In what seemed like a family room just off the kitchen, she sat to relax and enjoy the quiet around her because no one was upstairs. Maxwell walked out of the bathroom. He started to search for Charmin, finding her in the family room lounged on a sofa and deciding to join her and cool down. The silence soon turned into romantic talk about caring for each other and being patient while trying to understand how the other operated and thought. Maxwell turned to face her and asked her to kiss him, which she did with all of her heart.

The rage of passion evolved into tight hugs. He felt her body, and her hands wandered over his too, resting at the crotch of his jeans. She unzipped them and, for the first time, took his thick, long, rock-hard shaft out and into her mouth. He rested his head against the sofa top. She remembered closing her eyes and just doing what felt good and comfortable to her. She gave him her first intense, loving blow job, and he experienced for the first time having the rush of ejaculating into her mouth, which she swallowed hard and fast. They both smiled at each other as she held his shaft in her hands, gently pressing it against her face.

Back on the massage table, she was unaware of what Hank was doing; all she knew was that the feeling kept her relaxed and aroused. He asked her to turn over and placed a warm towel over her eyes in a coconut scent. She could feel the oil being applied to her breasts as he massaged each one. Before reaching for her stomach, he stopped to avoid her pubic area, where he also placed a towel. Both Maxwell and Charmin enjoyed their massages and vowed to continue receiving them back in the States.

Ten days had passed, bringing their honeymoon to an end, and they headed to the airport. He had to attend a business meeting in London, and she was heading to their new home in Washington, DC. They traveled together until San Juan, where they had to board separate flights.

Chapter 9

Later that evening, she wanted to share the experience she had had at the airport mall, so she texted him:

> I couldn't stop thinking about you, so I went into the ladies' room. I had to pee and then realized my panties were sticky wet from still thinking about you. I kicked my leg against the wall of the stall; my heels gave me traction. I held my other leg with my hand for balance. My back was pushed hard against a metal fixture. I couldn't help but bite my lips to quiet my moans as I abused my clitoris. I came so fast, I got a head rush, but I was able to focus for the remainder of the day. Hope your day was as good as mine.

Home, Sweet Home

Entering the house alone gave her an empty feeling, but knowing Maxwell would be home in a few days gave her an erotic feeling of being loved and understood. Too tired to unpack, she decided to take a shower. She stepped into the shower, and erotic memories filled her thoughts as she washed her hair and showered, allowing the stream of water to rinse over her body. Her mind felt free and uninhibited because of Maxwell before heading to bed by ten in the evening.

Charmin slept until about seven in the morning. She wandered into the kitchen to enjoy a cup of hot tea and to take in the morning light from the bay windows. She dressed and dashed off to the grocery store and then to Macy's for some quick shopping, returning by two in the afternoon, which allowed her to get some light housecleaning out of the way. This included vacuuming, dusting, and polishing the wooden flooring. She wasn't ready to tackle the suitcases alone, so she worked around them.

The doorbell rang out.

"Just a minute, I'm coming," she cried out.

Dressed in one of Maxwell's old sweatshirts and pair of shorts, she opened the door. There stood a voluptuous, tall, attractive woman, nicely dressed in a long sundress.

"Hello?"

"Um, hi, I'm sorry. I was looking for Max? Does he still live here?"

"If you mean Maxwell, yes, he does live here. That's my husband. Can I help you?"

"Oh, sorry, I didn't realize he married. We are old friends from a long time ago. Sorry for the awkward visit. I really didn't know."

"Well. We've lived together for almost five years. When was the last time you saw him?"

"Sorry, really it's an awkward mistake, and about five or so years ago. I had to leave town on business shortly after we met, so we didn't see each other again."

"That's odd. A one-night stand, and after five plus years, you are now looking for him?"

"Well, it really wasn't a one-night stand. We saw each other from time to time before I left town. Anyway, sorry for the awkward visit. Again, I didn't know. Good-bye."

"No. Wait! What is your name, so I can tell him you stopped by?"

"Tanya! Bye for now."

What? Charmin wondered. *"Bye for now"? What does that mean? Weird!*

Charmin watched as Tanya got into her car and drove off in a gray Acura TL. She tried not to make anything of it, realizing they both had lives—plus he did tell her he had slept around before she moved in.

Later that evening, Maxwell called. He seemed stressed and bothered because a deal that was in the works was not going as planned, and the need to extend his two-day trip seemed inevitable. Instead of adding to his stressful day, she decided not to mention Tanya until he got home.

Perhaps a little phone sex would help him relieve some stress, she thought to herself and proceeded to talk dirty. "I wish your dick was here right now. I would wrap my lips around it and suck you dry."

"Nice! Go on."

"I would lick the pre-cum off the tip of your shaft while cupping your balls in my hands."

"Really? I like that."

"I would take off my bra and slide your shaft between my large, full breasts up and down with long strokes. And suck the tip of your head each time it poked out."

"Ooh yeah! My dick is getting harder just hearing your voice. Make me cum, baby," he said.

"I want to sit on your dick and feel your hard thick shaft inside me, fucking me! Good and hard. While you suck on my nipples, I want you to spread me eagle-wide and thrust your shaft deep inside of me. I want to call out your name after you fuck me into an orgasm. I need and want your dick right now. My finger inside my pussy isn't you."

The sound of heavy moans echoed through the phone before

Maxwell ejaculated into a wet towel. Charmin knew her mission was a success. And Maxwell seemed relaxed and ready to tackle his challenges before returning home to physically fuck her.

"That was real nice, baby. I plan to fuck you good and hard when I get home. Be ready for my thick long shaft to spread you wide-open," he said. "Send me a picture of yourself."

Charmin reached for her digital camera sitting on the desktop, and while talking to Maxwell, spread her legs as wide as she could and photographed her center jewels.

"Got it," he said. "I'll sleep with a hard-on until I see you. I love you, babe."

"Me too," she said.

The light of the sun shined through the sheer drapes, waking Charmin at seven o'clock sharp. Remembering she was still home alone but that Maxwell would be back early tomorrow afternoon, she decided to make use of her time by writing thank-you cards and sorting through most of the wedding gifts. The kitchen was spacious, with a large center cooking station equipped with six burners, and the refrigerator was a custom-made, stainless-steel model with a temperate-control touch screen.

She went through the refrigerator and sorted out some of the fresh produce she had purchased the day prior to make herself a good breakfast of turkey sausage, fresh fruit, and homemade waffles on her new waffle maker. After cleaning up the kitchen, she decided to sort out her clothes that needed to be dry-cleaned or washed.

She returned phone calls to family members and close friends, letting them know they had returned from St. Barth's and were getting settled in their home. She really wanted to share all the erotic sexual experiences they had shared but decided against all the intimate details.

Instead, she made plans to meet her good friends at a nearby pub for drinks and light dinner to play catch-up. It was eight in the evening when she returned home from her outing, but felt so tired it seemed later. It occurred to her that perhaps she had had two martinis more than she should have enjoyed.

As she prepared for bed, a feeling of loneliness swept over her because Maxwell was not lying next to her with his tight embrace and loving kisses as sleep swept over her.

En route to the airport, Charmin was reflecting on the man she married and all the wild and erotic sex they had had in Saint Barthelemy. Three days had passed since they had seen each other last, and she wondered if the same adrenaline would be present in their new home. She approached the arrivals section and scanned the area for Maxwell.

There he was. Tall and handsome and dressed in jeans, a T-shirt, and a navy sports jacket, he stood out of the crowd. He immediately recognized her grey Porsche and "Sassy" tags. He waved with anticipation of seeing her. She had to wait to allow the flow of traffic to grant her the right of way, watching Maxwell move around in his fitted jeans.

He opened the back door and threw his luggage in the back, yelling, "Hey, babe!"

"Hey," she said. "Do you want to drive or not?"

He said, "No, I'm good. I'll let my woman drive me home. I've missed you, baby."

"Me too," she said.

Before sitting, he removed his sport jacket and hung it on the backside hook.

He leaned over and planted a deep, wet, passionate kiss on her lips while cupping her breasts. "I missed those, too."

She smiled and said, "Not for long."

He said, "I know. Let's get away from all this crazy traffic. I want to show you how much I've missed you."

As the traffic started to move, allowing space between each car and creating a distance from the airport, Maxwell looked at Charmin and took in her sexy outfit: white shorts and a grey tank top. From the shape of her breasts, she was wearing a sweetheart bra, revealing a glimpse of her breasts and nipples.

He reached over to her and lifted her tank top up while she was driving, exposing her black bra. Then he asked her to lean forward so he could unhook her strap. Her voice echoed, "The hooks are in the front, in between my breasts."

"Nice," he said.

With just one hand he unhooked her bra, freeing the voluptuous breasts he loved so much. With the same hand, he cupped her breasts, squeezing and pinching her nipples. She moaned quietly, letting him know she liked what he was doing.

He whispered, "Keep your eyes on the road and let me do what I need to do. Okay?"

And she said, "Okay."

He pressed his open mouth around her breast and started to suck on her breast and bite her nipple with strong suction, as if he were feeding.

Charmin felt his hands sliding down her stomach and rest in the warmth between her thighs. As he squeezed her groin, undoing the zipper and button seemed effortless, and his hands slid into her shorts panties, touching the warmth of her pubic skin before locating her lips, which he separated in search of her clitoris.

As he forced his hands farther underneath her, moisture was forming against his hands. He played with her clitoris while he sucked on her breasts. Charmin was finding it very hard to focus on the open road as cars, trucks, and buses passed them. The vision that was clear was what was happening to her. Maxwell continued to suck and lick each breast as he started to finger-fuck her slowly.

He sighed. "I need you to pull over so we can switch places." He pulled his fingers out of her canal and smelled them. "Ah. I missed that smell."

Charmin searched for a tourist rest stop area, which was about two miles up ahead. While he rested his head against the seat, his jeans were getting tighter. "My dick is rock hard," he said.

Pulling into the rest stop, Charmin searched for a discreet area because Maxwell had left her breasts exposed. She passed families and people walking their dogs to a remote parking area nearest the truck stops. As she started to park, Maxwell unzipped his jeans and released his long, thick shaft.

"It's ready for action," he said.

She eyed his dick and said, "Can't wait to have it in my mouth."

She flung her tank top over her head, slipped the bra off her shoulders, lowered her shorts to her knees, and bent forward toward Maxwell's dick. Arching her ass toward the window with her hips resting against the steering wheel, she hovered over the shift gears. Maxwell sank into the seat. As Charmin's mouth engulfed his shaft with deep sucks and heavy licks, drool escaped her mouth, dripping onto his balls.

She forced her face into his crotch, creating a deep-throat effect. This caused Maxwell to moan and adjust himself while he held her head and hair flush against his crotch. He was enjoying the blow job so much that he had lost sight of why they pulled over.

He reached over to her ass and spanked it. "I don't want to juice yet. Let's get home."

Charmin lifted her head up and said, "Do you still want to drive, or should I continue driving?"

He squeezed her breasts into her chest and said, "I can't wait to fuck you. I'll drive."

Still not fully dressed, Charmin switched places with Maxwell, but she did put on her tank top without the bra, her shorts, and her wet thong. He drove with his shaft exposed over his jeans, and she played with it. Charmin laid against Maxwell's shoulder while he drove them home for the first time since their wedding.

As they pulled into the driveway, Charmin reached for the garage door opener, and they pulled directly in. Neither wasted any time as the garage doors closed and the engine was silenced to embrace in a tight, wet kiss of "I love you" and "I missed you."

He reached under her tank top and squeezed her breasts. While they engaged in heated tongue kissing, he pulled her toward him, causing her to leap into his lap. She lifted her arms and he pulled off her tank top. Then he did the same as she pulled off his T-shirt, allowing for skin-to-skin contact. Maxwell retracted and lowered the seat, putting it in a flat position. He motioned to Charmin to help him remove his jeans and navy penny loafers while she slipped out of her shorts.

Confined in a tight front seat—the Porsche was a narrow car— he braced his knees, allowing Charmin to turn herself on her knees halfway up so she could position her knees to rest on his shoulders and her legs over his head creating a 69 position, while taking in his rock-hard shaft. Her hot wet mouth savored his shaft as a mouth-watering treat of heavy sucks. She licked his pre-cum as her head moved up and down over his shaft. Her tongue was dancing around his throbbing cock, giving Maxwell the full view of the opening of her canal, which he stuck his tongue down while rubbing her clitoris.

He finger-fucked her canal and created a deep suction against her clitoris, which caused Charmin to moan aloud. She tried to reach back to relieve his pressure, but she couldn't reach his face. Instead, her orgasm caused her to squirt juice in his face and mouth.

"Wow! That was too crazy. I loved it. You have a squirting pussy," he said, pleasantly shocked. "Let's get out of here. I need to fuck you."

Charmin slid off his face and onto the passenger seat to regain her balance before sitting up to exit the car. She stepped out and walked around the front toward the hood in search of a quilt or heavy blanket.

"What are you doing?" Maxwell asked.

"You'll see."

She reached for a large plastic bag containing bed quilts, unzipped it, removed two quilts, and placed them on the hood of the car, which was still very hot from the engine. She stared at Maxwell while she touched her sexy naked body.

"Nice," he said, but asked again, "What are you doing?"

She said, "I'd like you to fuck me on the hood of my car. Is that okay?"

"I could do that," he said.

She leaned forward toward the Porsche, pressing her breasts against the warm quilts, and spread her legs and arched her ass to allow Maxwell his favorite doggy-style position. She felt his hands slide under her and cup her very wet pussy to play with her clitoris, just before putting two of his fingers inside her very wet slit. He then started to finger-fuck her, and Charmin's body moved rhythmically against Maxwell's fingers. While finger-fucking Charmin, Maxwell started to stroke his shaft up and down, releasing more pre-cum before he exchanged his fingers for his thick, long dick. His dick entered Charmin hard and deep as he spanked her ass.

He started to fuck her like an animal in heat. Grabbing hold of her hair, he pulled his shaft out and sighed aloud, "Not yet." He placed his shaft back inside of Charmin and continued fucking her hard and fast again. He again pulled his shaft out and sighed. "Not yet. Let's go inside," he said in a demanding manner.

The garage doorway opened up into the mudroom. Maxwell swept Charmin off her feet and carried her through the house, stopping in front of the stairway. He placed her in front of the stairs and asked her to kneel on the fourth step and arch her back so he could position himself behind her on the third step, allowing him to fuck her doggy style. She did as he instructed, and he fucked her hard at times before shooting his sticky load inside of her wet pussy.

As an afterthought, he said, "Did you take your pill today?"

"I did."

They rummaged through the house and unpacked their suitcases before having a late dinner at their favorite restaurant, Michael's, which overlooked the bay. They enjoyed fresh soft-shell crab sandwiches and salt-and-pepper calamari along with a glass of wine. As they capped off their evening by taking a shower together, Maxwell recounted his London trip.

Charmin woke before Maxwell and decided to prepare a nice Sunday breakfast as a reminder that it was their first morning together in their home as newlyweds. This beautiful home had once belonged to only Maxwell when he accepted the vice president position at the construction company he had worked at for almost ten years.

Charmin still owned her condominium in Tampa, which she

decided to keep and rent as an investment. Most of the furniture had been purchased jointly except the king size bed, which she insisted be replaced prior to her moving in. She knew him well enough to know that not all of the sexual activities that had occurred on that bed were with her. Her philosophy was that a new bed allowed for new beginnings without lingering thoughts about the past. Interesting notion!

As she was preparing breakfast, Maxwell walked into the kitchen naked in search of her. He had a very apparent hard-on that required attention. She was wearing a sheer lace mini robe, which he was admiring as he walked toward her.

"Morning, babe," he said.

"Good morning, sweetie," she replied.

"I missed you this morning," he said.

"Really, what do you mean? Is there something in particular I can do for you?"

"Yes, there is, as a matter of fact."

"What's that?" she said.

"Well, love, I have a hard-on with your name on it."

"Nice! How do you want to handle that problem?" she teased.

"Well!" he exclaimed as he reached toward her and pulled the satin tie loose, causing her laced robe to fall open.

Her shaved pussy was immediately exposed, and he reached in and exposed her large voluptuous breasts before slipping the robe off her body. He cupped her breasts with a firm grip before taking her nipples into his mouth. He reached for her pussy with his other hand, gently separating her lips to feel for any moisture.

"Nice. You're wet."

"I'm always wet when you come near me," she said. He lowered himself while she held him for support. He placed his face between her thighs and inserted his tongue to lick some of the moisture.

"I'm hungry," his voice echoed.

"What are you hungry for?" she said.

"Your pussy!"

"I aim to please," she said.

She reached out to grab the center island for support while he lifted her up and placed her on the edge of the island, spreading her legs over his shoulders. He placed his face against her thighs, just smelling her natural pheromones, before slipping his finger inside her wet hole and starting to suck on her clitoris. His motion was slow yet forceful.

Charmin was experiencing mixed emotions because she realized the bacon and eggs were burning and the coffee machine was ringing, and all the while she was experiencing an orgasmic head rush.

His wet mouth moved from her clitoris to her breasts as he sucked and licked her nipples. He leaned forward, causing his rock-hard shaft to enter her cock socket as he began to thrust hard against her canal.

Charmin started to moan aloud, causing Maxwell to thrust harder. He held her with a strong, firm grip as he removed her from the island and elevated her against his chest. His hands moved down to support her ass as she pounded against his hard shaft at an elevated angle. He moved toward the kitchen wall as he pushed her back into the wall. Her legs climbed high against his waist, welcoming every pound into her pussy.

Charmin was enjoying the sexual pleasure Maxwell was giving her before calling out, "I want you to cum in my mouth. I haven't wrapped my lips around your thick long meat pole this morning. Let me swallow your hot sticky load, Maxwell!" she said.

Maxwell allowed her to slip off his shaft onto her knees before placing his shaft, covered in her juice, in her mouth. As he looked down at her sucking on his shaft, he could feel his stream ready to surface.

"Are you ready, baby? I have a thick load ready to juice in your mouth."

He held his shaft while in her mouth. Within a moment of completing his words, his load exploded in her mouth. Charmin was swallowing quickly. Before he removed his shaft, which was still spurting juice, he aimed it at her face and said, "Open wide and close your eyes." Juice landed on her nose and chin, giving her a sperm facial.

He tugged at his shaft to ensure all the juice was out, and a small amount of remaining juice spilled from it. Charmin reached over to his dick and stuck out her tongue to lick his excess drops. Maxwell enjoyed watching her use her tongue to lick his every drop.

Chapter 10

Breakfast had been ruined, so they decided to head out for brunch at a local restaurant in Georgetown. Maxwell ordered homemade waffles with maple syrup and bacon, while Charmin ordered a cheese omelet with bacon and chilled cranberry juice.

During brunch, Maxwell asked if she had made any plans for the day because he wanted to take a drive to the eastern shore and visit a good friend. Charmin had no plans, only to hang out with her man. After brunch, they headed out toward the Maryland shore; the bay bridge seemed open, which was rare, as traffic was common.

Maxwell wanted to visit a friend who owned a golf course and had not been able to attend their wedding. They had been friends for many years, so Charmin realized her day would be spent at a country club.

The main entrance offered grandness with its beautiful pruned shrubs and bright-colored flowers that adorned the driveway and landscape leading to the front door. There was an excess of people young and old moving all about the premises as Maxwell parked his blue BMW.

Maxwell reached for his cell and placed a call to his friend, letting him know they had arrived. A slim gentleman still on his own phone walked out, waving toward Maxwell.

"Hey, man. How's it going?" he said.

"Dude, I'm good!" Maxwell said. "Do you remember Charmin, my sexy wife?"

"I do. Hello," he said as he extended his hand to greet her, "I'm Nick."

"Hello, Nick," she said.

"Let's head in. There are a few folks I'd like you all to meet."

They reached the foyer, where a dozen or so folks were conversing. Nick motioned to a few guys to come over and he introduced each of them. Maxwell seemed to be in his element. Meanwhile, Charmin was searching about to see if she recognized any women in the crowd.

Instead, a very attractive woman started walking toward them, greeting her husband before saying, "Hi, I'm Jaz, his wife." She pointed to one of the guys in the group.

"Hello. I'm Charmin."

"Want to walk with me while the guys shoot the shit?"

"Yeah, sounds good."

As they were walking away, Charmin could feel Maxwell watching them.

"Thanks for rescuing me back there," Charmin said. "It was getting a little boring listening to golf talk and automobiles."

"Yeah, I'm not surprised," Jaz said. "So anyway, I have a few friends waiting for me at the bar. Want to join us?"

"Okay."

The bar area seemed packed with people, which made Charmin wonder why they weren't playing golf. Instead, most of them were getting buzzed from beer and cocktails. She thought to herself, *When in Rome,* ordered a blueberry martini, and settled in with her new friends. All of them were married but one who was in the process of a divorce and was recounting why men would cheat—it was always about sex, wasn't it? Charmin just listened as everyone seemed to concur with the woman's observation.

Then Jaz said, "We all have to keep a spark in our sex lives or they will search outward. Micky and I have decided to become swingers. I know it sounds crazy, but it works for us. There is something erotic and exciting about meeting someone you are attracted too and then fucking them, knowing your husband is watching. While we were in Amsterdam, one of the craziest, sexy things I've experienced was joining a threesome with a husband and wife. They just wanted to fuck each other. Then they saw Micky and me and asked if I could join them for a night of fun. They reserved a room that had mirrors and a verse window. As we walked toward the room, all I could feel were hands touching me. I really enjoyed that experience. Maybe one day I'll tell you guys all about it."

Jaz was a very attractive woman with good height. Her body was voluptuous by nature, and her attitude supported her appearance. Charmin looked at Jaz with a feeling of understanding because she knew she also had to make adjustments to keep Maxwell satisfied, and now she felt assured she wasn't the only married woman thinking that way.

One of the other ladies, Cindy, had good height as well with a slim build but perfect breasts. She mentioned that as much as she didn't care for the taste of cum in her mouth, she needed to learn to enjoy swallowing her husband's spunk because it offended him when she spit it out. Even though it wasn't her thing, she thought that keep harmony in her home started with a sexual balance.

Cindy was married to Nick. Her appearance was very conservative, and yet her husband enjoyed watching women who dressed risqué. They all smiled as they arrived at a general understanding that the needs and wants of men appeared greater than most women's.

Charmin interjected, "The many needs of the one dominate." She laughed at herself but reflected on the meaning.

Lauren, who was getting a divorce, said she had caught her husband at her neighbor's home. They appeared to be about the same age, except the woman had breast implants and a large ass, whereas Lauren was slim and petite. She thought the woman's body had enticed her husband because he'd asked her to get implants a few years before. This woman had no problem telling Lauren that her husband enjoyed watching her lick at her own nipples and then titty-fucking her before shooting his load against her breast. They had seldom fucked because he enjoyed fucking his wife—her, Lauren. She was clearly sad as she shared her experience.

"I'm not sure what to do," she said. No one offered advice because only she could decide whether to accept his ways and get implants or just leave him.

Beth chimed in next. "My husband likes when I greet him at the door naked. He gets mad when I forget to meet him at the door with no clothes. He likes when I take his briefcase from him and place it on the hall table. As I'm laying it on the table, I arch my ass so he can spank me hard. Then I say, 'Thank you, babe,' before he would either fuck me or I would give him a welcome-home blow job to start his evening."

One of the other women in the group, Maggie, said, "Well, ladies, mine enjoys watching me masturbate as part of our foreplay, which gets him off so he can fuck me like a horny man should." Laughter rang out amongst all of the women.

Charmin didn't feel like sharing any intimate secrets, but, offering a smile of naughtiness, she did say, "Maxwell really enjoys sex."

Maxwell and a group of guys entered the bar area in search of their wives. Finding one allowed them to find all of them. Charmin glanced at Maxwell to gauge his mood as he stared back at her with a wink.

"So, ladies, what are we drinking?" Nick asked. He ordered a round of beer and vodka shots.

Maxwell made his way to Charmin to share her ottoman-like chair while the others collected chairs to add to their circle.

"Hey, baby, what are you guys talking about?" Maxwell asked.

"Men and sex—what else?" she said.

"Nice!" he replied.

Charmin leaned into him and asked, "Any of these women giving you a hard-on?"

"No, baby. Only you!" he said. "I like the way your nipples stick out," as he brushed his hands against her fitted top.

"My nipples get hard because you excite me whenever you're near me. I already feel my panties getting sticky wet because you touched my nipples."

Maxwell said, "Nice! We'll have to take care of that. I think you should come with me to the unisex bathroom near the entrance hallway."

Maxwell excused the couple from the circle and said, "We will be back shortly."

Having overheard the conversation, Jaz smiled at Charmin and said, "Your seats will be waiting for you."

Taking her hand, Maxwell led Charmin toward the unisex bathroom, which was occupied, so they waited in the hall. Maxwell stood in front of her and pressed his hand against her mini skirt. As he reached under it, he touched her panties and confirmed a wet sticky substance was present. His finger to slipped past her panties and into inside her now very wet pussy, gently finger-fucking her. Charmin was becoming very aroused with each stroke before embracing him in a passionate kiss. Charmin spread her legs a little wider to show him how much she was enjoying the invasion of his finger and wanted more. A click at the bathroom door sounded before it opened.

Maxwell instantly slipped his hands from under her skirt, embracing her waist and stepping beside her, ready to enter the bathroom. The door had barely shut before Maxwell held Charmin in a tight embrace, asking her to tell him what she wanted him to do.

Charmin, in a throaty voice, said, "I want you to stick your dick inside my pussy—fuck me until I cum all over your dick."

Maxwell smiled, reached under her miniskirt, rolled her panties down her legs, and lifted each leg to remove them. He then hiked up her skirt while she unzipped his pants and freed his shaft for action. He leaned her against the bathroom wall and elevated one of her legs for easy access.

Maxwell's shaft was rock hard as he shoved it inside her canal, fucking her as if they hadn't fucked that morning. Each thrust caused him to moan, "Your pussy feels so good against my dick. Oh, baby, I'm going to juice inside you." Then he burst out in a grinding voice, "Oh yeah!"

He pressed his lips against hers and said, "Thank you for this. I was just horny."

He then reinserted his dick back inside his pants and lowered Charmin's skirt, asking her not to put her panties back on—instead, he slipped them into his pocket. Charmin looked in the mirror to refresh her makeup and hair, and Maxwell watched her before kissing the back of her neck.

"You look beautiful. Let's go," he said.

About thirty minutes had passed since they'd left for the bathroom, causing Nick to ask if everything was okay. Maxwell responded, "Everything is good, man—thanks for asking."

Jaz looked over at Charmin, who smiled and said, "We do what we have to do—right, ladies?" All the women around the lounge table cheered and said, "Absolutely," causing the men to wonder what had happened before they joined them. Nonetheless, everyone was having a good time.

Maxwell was getting hungry and wanted to order food, so everyone decided to share appetizers of lobster balls, clam casinos, and oysters on the half shell laced with hot sauce, lemon juice, and vodka.

Charmin wanted to head back—the next day was her first day back in the office after being gone for fifteen days. She nudged Maxwell to see if he was ready to go because they had a two-hour drive home and it was already six in the evening.

Maxwell responded, "If you are ready! We can go."

She said, "Okay."

Charmin said her good-byes as they all exchanged cell numbers and planned to get together soon.

On the drive home, Maxwell thanked Charmin for being a good sport, not having known she would be at a country club all day.

Charmin said, "I'm game with whatever you want to do. We are free and in love, so that's what we should expect from each other. Besides, I don't want to be anywhere you are not."

"We have too much fun together—out-of-the-box sex, good company, and cool new friends," she continued. I'll always remember Katlyn. I'm sure you'll remember her too." Maxwell smiled. "I think Jaz and I are going to keep in touch. I like the way she thinks and how she handles obstacles."

"What do you mean?" Maxwell asked.

"Oh, nothing," Charmin said. "She's a cool person."

"Okay," he said.

The drive seemed long, and traffic was at a standstill, so Charmin looked over at Maxwell and said, "I'm getting tired. Do you need me to stay up with you, or can I take a nap?"

"Take a nap, baby. I'm good," he said.

"I also want to invite Nick and Cindy and Jaz and Micky over for dinner and drinks soon—well, maybe the whole gang. I really enjoyed everyone's company. What do you think?"

"I think it's a good idea," he said.

Charmin closed her eyes for what seemed like just a few minutes only for Maxwell to wake her as he reached for the garage door opener and pulled into the garage.

"Oh, sorry, I passed out."

He reached over to her, kissed her, and said, "It's okay."

They entered the house, and Charmin walked upstairs to take a shower and get ready for bed. Maxwell checked his e-mail before joining her and snuggled in bed with her.

Maxwell said, "My fingers still smell like you."

"Really?" she said.

"I love you, babe."

"I love you too. Although you should wash your hands and face before going to bed," she said lovingly.

He reached under her and said, "I want to sleep with my finger inside of you."

Charmin just smiled and closed her eyes.

Chapter 11

The sound of the alarm radio pulled Charmin back to reality as it played out the loud voice of a news commentator discussing the economy and coming elections. Maxwell reached over and turned the alarm off to continue sleeping while Charmin jetted off the bed to prepare for her return to work. She was an early bird, whereas Maxwell was a night owl. This sometimes created an imbalance between them, but compromise and patience became their virtues. Sometimes she would occupy her time by painting her nails to allow Maxwell time to sleep or by reading and writing.

Brushing the sleep from her face, Charmin stretched her body to awake her senses while taking account of the man lying next to her. Their bedroom was painted a light mauve-brown and featured three very large windows covered with decorated window treatments. A white ceiling fan hung high because of the vaulted ceilings.

The master suite was spacious in size with one large walk-in closet and a bathroom with a soak-in Jacuzzi and shower stall fit for two. She jumped in the shower, allowing the cool water to wash over her body and jolt energy into her soul. With light makeup and an up-do hairstyle, she put on a skirt suit and strap-on sandals. Charmin hurried along so as not to be late her first day back and kissed Maxwell goodbye while he smiled, returning to sleep. She prepared a light fruit breakfast along with egg whites, grabbed a cup of orange juice, and dashed out the door.

Her drive seemed long and boring compared to her wild, erotic honeymoon. Thirty minutes later, as she perused her schedule for the day, things seemed back to normal: a hectic day filled with back-to-back meetings and short suspense—everything always seemed like an emergency. She conversed with her colleagues about the island of Saint Barth's and recommended that everyone experience the island at least once.

"Hey, Charmin. Welcome back. We are all gathering in the boardroom for a short meeting in five minutes. I'm not sure what the topic is, but Tom and Ned are already in their offices, which is pretty early for them. See ya there."

"Thanks, Tanya. I'll be there in a minute." *Tanya!* Charmin immediately thought. *I forgot to mention Tanya to Maxwell—darn!*

Before heading to the boardroom, Charmin jotted a note for herself to tell Maxwell about Tanya's visit when she got home.

Maxwell, meanwhile, had the opportunity to sleep in because he had a fifteen-minute drive to the office. He called Charmin to see how she was doing on her first day back as a married woman. Charmin glanced at the number before she answered, her voice hinted that she was happy to hear from him, and she smiled to herself, recounting all they had experienced together. He said that his day didn't seem too busy and suggested that they plan something for dinner around 7:00 p.m. He'd call her back.

"Honey, I forgot to mention you had a visitor while you were in London. Maxwell?"

While on the phone with Charmin, Maxwell noticed a car moving too fast in the thirty-five-miles-per-hour zone before rear-ending another car. The impact was incredibly loud and hard, but no one appeared to be hurt. Traffic came to a standstill, which meant, unfortunately, that his fifteen-minute drive just had gotten longer. So instead of sitting idle, he shared the incident before disconnecting with Charmin, who missed the chance to mention Tanya. He wanted to contact his office to hold a telecom staff meeting. Charmin realized Maxwell did not hear what she had said and decided they would have to talk later.

"Good morning, everyone. I'm stuck in traffic, so let's go over today's schedule."

"Hey, Maxwell, welcome back! How was your honeymoon?" a voice shouted over the phone.

"Good. Really good. I've married a wonderful woman and can't be any happier. Thanks for asking," Maxwell replied. "So I've sent over my notes from the London trip—looks like the deal is on track. Let's plan another visit by the end of the month as a follow-up. Sam and George, let's get together when I get into the office. I want to review the schematics that were presented at the meeting in London."

"Sure thing, boss," George responded.

Almost thirty-five minutes later, Maxwell entered the office and met with George and Sam. The meeting was brief and productive.

Sitting in his office, Maxwell started searching the Internet on his iPhone for a nice restaurant in the area and instead noticed an advisement for women's undergarments. This made him think of purchasing a gift for Charmin. His search quickly turned to Victoria's Secret and then Frederick's of Hollywood before coming across vibrating panties.

This enticed his appetite, so he contacted a local novelty shop and purchased a vibrating thong he offered an extra thirty dollars if the driver could have it delivered to his office by three in the afternoon. Excited and filled with anticipation, he made dinner reservation at a new DC restaurant, knowing his motives were sexual. Then, he called Charmin to tell her he had made reservations for dinner at a new restaurant for seven in the evening. For the rest of the day, Maxwell was uneasy, anxiously thinking about sex. He was incredibly impatient when it came time to do something he wanted to do—sex especially.

At three in the afternoon, his anxiety grew more intense. Finally his package arrived. He collected his box and dashed back to his office. He eagerly opened it, revealing a thong, a battery box, and a chrome-like egg. He quickly visualized Charmin wearing them. Charmin was in the middle of a conference call when Maxwell called her, so she muted it to receive his call. He seemed anxious and eager to see her. She couldn't help but wonder what was going on with him. She knew him well enough to realize he was up to something.

As a lead account manager for a real estate company, Charmin was confined to meetings and conference calls. She supervised eight people and enjoyed the camaraderie she received at work, but her days were sometimes very long. Maxwell was the vice president of a large construction company in the middle of designing and constructing a new three-level mall, so his days were also spent in meetings and conference calls and traveling locally and abroad, but his workdays fluctuated from short to long, depending on current events.

On her drive home from work, Charmin remembered him sharing an experience he had had abroad in an establishment similar to an American gentlemen's club and yet very different. The gentlemen's club had women and men wearing masquerade masks and very revealing clothing. Both the women and men were in control and enjoyed sexual freedom, including submissive and dominant roles.

Many of the women were very attractive and flaunted their bodies for show, leaving nothing to the imagination. Maxwell, along with a colleague, entered the establishment to experience how other cultures enjoyed sex. Many women greeted him and his colleague, who were then escorted by the two of their choice, who sat them at a table and kneeled next to them submissively, awaiting a command. The women would wait by their sides to serve drinks and food to them.

An attractive woman caught Maxwell's eye as she offered her body to him, but he declined. He instead only wanted to experience an oral sensation. This very thin, tall, and full-breasted woman led him into an open room, exposing other men having sexual encounters.

The woman led him to a bench-like chair. Then she disrobed, got on her knees, and unzipped his pants to expose his dick, which she then started to swallow. As Maxwell was enjoying his oral pleasure, he was able to watch his colleague, who had opted to have sex with multiple women. Two of the women were sucking his dick while another was sitting on his face.

Maxwell enjoyed watching the two women sexually play with each other. The woman who was servicing him had some skills. She was so in tune that she knew when he was ready to ejaculate, so just before he did, she took his dick out of her mouth and said, "I'd like you to come on my face." Having his hot cum splash all over her face reinforced how much he enjoyed giving sperm facials.

As she reflected, Charmin realized that all around the world, sexual gratification was played out in many different ways. Men's needs really weren't different from women's. Only the approach gave men an edge because women, either for appearances' sake or by choice, didn't flaunt their sexual needs as men did. Instead, they exercised discretion.

She took herself as an example. By day, she was a professional workingwoman, and by night, she became an uninhibited sexual woman ready for anything. Meeting Maxwell in her youth certainly had a lot to do with her embracing her sexual freedom, and her love for him made it that much easier.

As she pulled into the driveway, she noticed Maxwell was already home. In her excitement, she rushed into the house in search of him, but he wasn't anywhere to be found. Then she heard his voice and realized he was on the phone in the den, so she went upstairs to shower and change for dinner. Searching through her clothes to find something to wear, she picked a sleeveless dress with a deep V to accent her breasts.

Charmin undressed and stepped into the shower to rinse off the day. As she was lathering her body, she heard Maxwell's voice saying hello and that he had something for her. As she stepped out of the shower and bathroom, she glimpsed at a box that was on the bed. Still wet from her shower, she walked toward the bed, only for Maxwell to intercept with a bear hug and kiss.

"Missed you so much today," he said.

"Me too," she said.

"I would like you to wear this tonight for me—okay?"

"What is it?" she said. Maxwell handed the box to Charmin, who was still naked from her shower. As he admired her body, she had started to open the box when she felt Maxwell cup her breasts and pinch her nipples.

"What's this?" she said. "A black thong?"

Maxwell said, "Not just a thong—a *vibrating* thong."

"Really? I've never owned one."

"Wow. Okay."

She took the black thong out, along with the battery box, wireless remote, and chrome-like egg, unsure of what to do with it. Maxwell read the instructions: they had to place the chrome egg into the battery box to charge for thirty to forty minutes. It was five in the afternoon, giving it plenty of time to charge before Charmin could wear it to dinner.

Maxwell said, "I want to fuck you so badly because I'm so horny just at the thought of you wearing this vibrating thong for me. It makes my shaft hard, but I want to wait until tonight."

Charmin smiled at Maxwell as she pressed herself against him and said, "I'd like to purchase a butt plug. Can you take me to a sex shop?"

Without hesitation he said, "Let's go!"

Maxwell took Charmin to a local sex shop, where they scouted out a butt plug for her, along with a tall bottle of lubricant. Walking through the shop introduced a wide variety of fun activities to try. She watched Maxwell grinning to his heart's content.

He grabbed a long-handled whip and smiled. "I like this."

"Really? What would you do with it?"

"I'd have you bend over and spank that ass of yours."

"Interesting."

There were so many different styles and shapes of both dildos and butt plugs. Maxwell pointed to a cobalt-blue plug, and she agreed it was a good, playful size for her, not too thick or long. Within thirty minutes, they were returning home, Charmin admiring her new purchase and Maxwell sporting a hard-on.

She rushed into the house and marched up the stairs in anticipation as she unpacked her purchase and started to wash it.

She turned toward Maxwell and said, "I think we are going to need some lubricant for my new butt plug."

"NICE!"

Charmin positioned herself on all fours and arched her back to expose her ass. Maxwell returned with the tall bottle of lubricant as he joined her on the bed, still wearing his clothes.

"I love your ass."

"Thank you. Hey, do you remember an old flame named Tanya?"

"No."

He poured the lubricant on her asshole before inserting the three-inch butt plug in her asshole. He played with the plug, moving it in and out of Charmin asshole. He enjoyed watching her body take it in and push it out, giving off a suction sound.

He helped her off the bed. Still wearing the plug, Charmin walked to the bathroom and proceeded to comb her hair and apply her makeup. Maxwell watched her move around the room with the cobalt-blue base of the plug sticking out of her ass.

Maxwell decided to change into a fresh shirt for a more casual appearance while Charmin slipped into a black sleeveless dress that accented her large breasts. One hour later, Maxwell took the chrome egg out of the charger box, placed it in his hands with the wireless remote, and turned it on.

The dial read on, low, medium, and high. As he tried each setting, the egg started to vibrate in his hands, creating a trembling sensation.

"Cool. I think it's ready for you to wear."

Charmin reached for the thong and placed the egg in the crotch sleeve. Maxwell helped her put her new thong on so the plug wouldn't slip out of her asshole. She was sexually ready and comfortable with the butt plug and the chrome-like egg wedged against her clitoris. Maxwell couldn't help but smile.

"Let's try it!"

"Okay," she said.

He turned the dial on, and Charmin felt a vibration, causing her to jolt in place.

He turned the dial to low, and instantly Charmin felt a sensation on her clitoris similar to Maxwell's fingers. The dial was a little more intense on medium, this time similar to his tongue, and then the last dial was high. "Okay, that's too much." It seemed past sensation and into hard intensity.

"Nice," he said. "I'll try and remember that."

"Try, really hard to remember that!" she said.

Chapter 12

On the drive to the restaurant, Maxwell turned the dial to low to watch Charmin's reaction.

She was glaring at him with a smile and said, "That feels nice."

She rested her head against the seat and touched her breasts as warmth spread across her body. She could feel the wetness forming between her thighs and against the vibrating egg. Because the ride was thirty minutes in length, the constant simulation against her clitoris caused the wetness to reach her dress. Since her dress was black, any wet stain would not be noticeable. But by the time they reached the restaurant, her breathing was getting a little heavy, and as she stepped out of the car, wetness was trickling down her thighs and legs.

She reached for Maxwell's hands and whispered in his ear, "I'm so wet; it's dripping out of me."

Maxwell and Charmin entered the restaurant together. Maxwell watched Charmin, who seemed distracted while they waited to be seated. Her facial expression revealed that she was very horny but unable to relieve the desire, and it made her very anxious. Maxwell couldn't help but turn the dial to medium as her eyes widened and focused on him.

"What's wrong?" he said, smiling.

She whispered, "I'm having an orgasm."

"Nice!"

"I've never had one in a restaurant surrounded by people before. Oh, Maxwell! I can't control myself." She moaned quietly while her body gave off an orgasmic movement like a floppy fish.

As she tried to regain her composure, she felt the added moisture against her thong start to stream down her thighs again. Maxwell enjoyed watching her and didn't care who else had witnessed her orgasm. He turned off the dial, remembering she was capable of having multiple orgasms.

He leaned into her and kissed her lips and said, "I love you more each day, if that's even possible."

As they sat at the table, Charmin tried to position herself so not to cause the butt plug to slip out since she was wearing a thong. Maxwell seemed poised and excited. Knowing what was going on with her excited him a great deal. The thong was saturated with wetness and sticky cum that was both against her pussy and streaming down her thighs from her recent orgasm, so she decided to retreat to the ladies' room.

Maxwell stared at her as she moved from the table toward the restroom. He admired her ass and shape in the dress, knowing she was wearing a plug up her ass. His trousers were getting tight as his shaft hardened against it just thinking about Charmin. She entered the bathroom stall and looked down at her legs to see the cream-like stream running down her legs. She wiped off the excess cum juice against her legs and settled against her thong. She realized she would have a cream-like cum stain against her new black thong by the end of dinner because of the vibrating egg wedged against her groin.

When she returned to the table, her breasts seemed full and perky. Maxwell almost wanted to reach out and grab them, but remembering where he was kept him in check. While they were enjoying their broccoli and steak dinner along with a shared piece of key lime pie drizzled with raspberry preserves, Charmin brought up the topic of Tanya again.

"Hey, are you sure you don't remember an old girlfriend named Tanya?"

"No. Why should I remember an old girlfriend when I have a beautiful wife I enjoy fucking sitting across from me?"

"That was sweet. But your old flame stopped by while you were in London."

"What? When? What did she want?"

"I don't know! You, I guess, although she did seem surprised that we were married."

"Well, I'm glad you told her I'm off the market so she won't make that mistake again. I haven't seen any old flames since you moved in almost five years ago. I can't remember—oh, wait. There was a Tanya about five or so years ago. She was a stewardess and was reassigned out to San Diego or Sacramento—somewhere in California. We only hung out a few times—nothing serious, just good old-fashioned fucking," he said, smiling.

"Well, you must have left a good impression on her for her to want to see you after all these years. You have quite a powerful dick, no doubt." Interesting that you've left such a lasting impression with her!

"Okay. This is not a cool topic. That was my past, and you are clearly my present and future."

"Smooth talker, but I love you anyway."

"I love you too, babe," he replied.

After dinner, Maxwell and Charmin left the restaurant feeling free and sexually uninhibited. In the car, Maxwell turned the dial on low to remind Charmin what was to follow as Charmin moaned quietly to herself, feeling very horny and ready to have his shaft inside her. Maxwell unzipped his trousers and freed his shaft. As Charmin reached over and took him in her mouth, sucking and licking, her head started moving up and down against the steering wheel.

As Maxwell drove and enjoyed his oral sensation, he reached

over to Charmin and pulled her dress over her ass, exposing the vibrating thong and visible butt plug base, and spanked her ass. Then he reached under the thong to finger her pussy, his finger surrounded by wetness as he finger-fucked her. He motioned her to stop to keep from ejecting his load in her mouth.

Charmin repositioned herself back to the passenger side and then lowered her dress. Maxwell smiled at her, saying, "I want to fuck you so bad it hurts my dick to think about it."

Charmin smiled and said, "You are all the man I need and want."

Maxwell parked in the driveway instead of the garage. They walked into the house, and Maxwell reached under Charmin's dress and started to lift it up and over her head. Charmin wasn't wearing a bra, so her large, full, perky breasts were exposed instantly. As Maxwell positioned himself behind her, he cupped and squeezed her breasts and nipples. His hands slid past her stomach and inside her panties, her breathing heavy and anxious.

Charmin turned to face him. As they embraced in a wet, passionate kiss, Charmin lowered herself to her knees, removed Maxwell's belt and unzipped his trousers. He enjoyed wearing Jordan briefs. He kicked off his loafers and removed his trousers and briefs, leaving just his dress shirt on. Charmin engulfed his shaft while firmly gripping his balls, and he held her head and hair as his hips moved in a fucking motion against her mouth.

Charmin decided to insert her finger inside Maxwell's asshole to share the feeling of sexual gratification. His moans confirmed he enjoyed the feeling. Maxwell then reached under her and lifted her to her feet. As he moved her toward the plush sofa and leaned her lower back against the arm of the sofa. He aggressively removed the vibrating thong saturated with her juice and moisture. He then got on his knees. He parted her lips, exposing her clitoris, which he took into his mouth while inserting his finger inside her well at the same time.

Charmin's body danced with an orgasmic rhythm. Maxwell lifted one of her legs, placing it over his shoulder as he continued to suck on her clitoris while finger-fucking her. Charmin's body shook with orgasms as she cupped and squeezed her breasts in delight. Maxwell stood up and turned her around, causing her to hunch over the sofa arm as he spread her legs and inserted his rock-hard shaft inside her hot, wet hole.

Giving her the feeling of double penetration was becoming a regular experience between them, as he moved the plug in and out of her asshole while fucking her in a hard rhythm. Maxwell removed his shaft to keep from releasing his juice too soon. He started to spank Charmin on the ass while he removed and reinserted the butt plug. Charmin was beside herself with ecstasy.

Maxwell decided he wanted to fuck Charmin in the ass with his dick, so he removed the plug, held it in his hands, and directed his shaft toward her asshole. She motioned for him to put on a condom because she knew he still wanted to fuck her in her pussy, and she knew her chocolate shoot carried bacteria that would give her an infection in her pussy. Maxwell understood. He left the room and returned with a box of condoms. He took out a Magnum Trojan and slipped it over his rock-hard shaft before gently sticking his dick in her asshole. Charmin could feel the difference in not only size but also length as she reached back and spread her cheeks to allow the entry.

Maxwell applied gentle pressure as her asshole, creating a suction-like feeling around his dick. The tightness was incredible, so he applied little movement before the full length of his shaft was deep inside her asshole. He elevated his leg to position it on the corner of the sofa arm, allowing for a firm grip of her ass before he started to move against her chocolate shoot, fucking her gently as the suction loosened.

He moved faster, and he realized he was fucking her with hard, deep thrusts and a tighter sensation. Charmin started to moan aloud as she reached under her body to rub her clitoris, which helped ease the pressure against her asshole before she experienced another orgasm.

Maxwell gently pulled his shaft from inside Charmin's asshole. The suction was great enough to milk his juice out, which he was not ready to do. Instead, Maxwell motioned toward the sofa and lay across it, looking at Charmin, who was still hunched over the arm.

"I'd like you to sit on my long, fat dick for a little while."

"Okay."

She stood up and walked toward Maxwell, removing the condom from his dick as she straddled him with her ass in front of his face. She gently sat on his rock-hard shaft, the sofa large enough to allow both of them to lie across it comfortably.

As her body was thrusting hard against his dick, Maxwell reached forward to hold her ass as it moved up and down. Again holding the butt plug, he decided to place it back inside of her asshole while he enjoyed the view of seeing both holes occupied. Charmin lifted herself from Maxwell's dick and took it in her mouth with deep sucks while giving him a closer view of her ass, which he gladly started to spank before she returned to sitting on his dick.

Maxwell asked Charmin to say out loud, "I like when you stick your dick inside my pussy," and she did. He started spanking her hard before succumbing to his orgasm as his heavy ejaculation flowed inside her canal. Both of them felt complete and happy as she lay back against Maxwell in a loving embrace, still wearing the plug.

Charmin realized his shaft had never been inside her asshole before, and she had enjoyed it so much that she wanted to have him fuck her ass again—but she knew that once he ejaculated, it took a few hours for him to revive himself.

Instead, Charmin said, "I think my asshole needs a break. It's time to take the butt plug out."

Maxwell reached over her and removed the plug from her asshole, causing a suction sound, and wetness flowed out of her asshole.

"Wow, what an experience," she said.

"Oh, baby. I think there will be a lot more of these experiences between us," he said. "Not only because I love fucking your tight, wet twat and your even tighter asshole, but also because you give stellar blow jobs. Plus, you are cool with the idea of letting another woman suck me off. What more can a man ask for? You are my prized possession. I know—within reason." He smiled.

Maxwell wrapped his arms around Charmin and said, "You are the woman that I need and want. I'm a lucky man to have found you."

Chapter 13

A week later, Charmin was lounging around the house when the front door slammed loudly.

"Maxwell, is everything okay? What's wrong?" she cried out.

There was an eerie silence that made her leap off the sofa in search of Maxwell. She rushed to her feet and roamed through each room until she spotted him looking out the window. He seemed far away and incredibly agitated.

"Babe, what is going on? Are you okay?"

The silence grew sickening. Finally, she reached for his arms and forced him to look at her. They locked eyes, but nothing was being transmitted from Maxwell.

"Sweetie, you are really scaring me. Please talk to me." Her eyes started to well with tears and she turned away.

"Charmin, please don't cry. I really can't handle that too."

"What does that mean? 'Too'! Talk to me."

Maxwell motioned toward the center of the room while reaching for her hands.

"I have something very serious to tell you. I need a drink or something first."

"You have never said that before. You need a drink? Because you can only focus if you have a drink in your hands when did you start that and nothing should be that difficult to tell me. So let's just sit down and relax. Take your time and just tell me what happened. Okay?"

"Okay. I'm really sorry for what I'm about to tell you. I love you."

"Sorry about what?"

"Well, after work today, I was pulling out of the parking lot when this car stopped behind me and a woman stepped out of her car and approached me."

"Tanya?"

"Yes!"

"Go on."

Maxwell lost his composure and started to cry uncontrollably as he placed his head between his legs for comfort. Charmin tried to console him, but he reluctantly isolated himself as if for protection.

"Please don't push me away. I can't handle that," she said.

"I'm sorry, baby. I'm sorry."

Maxwell tightly embraced his wife while sobbing in her arms. She had never seen him cry before, let alone lose control as if the problem was greater than him. This scared Charmin more than anything because whatever had happened had had an impact on their lives. She still didn't know what that impact was, but she was so afraid to hear what it was since it had clearly devastated Maxwell.

"Just breathe, sweetie. Please!"

"She told me that she had two kids, a boy and girl—twins—and that I was the father." He gave off a blink stare.

"What? What the hell? Two kids, and you didn't know?" Charmin stood up and stared down at her husband.

"How old are they, Maxwell?"

Maxwell looked up at Charmin with sadness and reached for her hands for support. But she did not extend them to him, instead giving him a hard stare.

"How old?"

"I did not know! We fucked a few times and she said she was on the pill and they are five years old."

"We have been together for over ten years and been living together for four years and six months. So three months before I moved in, Tanya was pregnant with your kids, and you didn't know that. Please don't take me for a fool. That would make me really angry! Why weren't you wearing a condom? Because you and I were fucking without a condom for over ten years! We were both tested before we got married, but you endangered both our lives by being promiscuous. I don't know what to say."

"I am so sorry for being so careless and irresponsible knowing all along I wanted you to be my wife and the mother of my children. I can't understand how you feel, but I am hurting too. This is not what I wanted for us—and with a stranger I only knew for a month or two. I'm so disgusted with myself and the situation."

"Are you going to take a paternity test to validate her accusation?"

"Yes, of course I will."

"If the test is positive, we'll do the right thing and jointly raise them because they are a part of you and we are married."

"Thank you. I love you, Charmin. I am so sorry for changing our plans for the future, and instead I'm asking you to help me raise another woman's kids. I am so sorry, baby. I have an appointment in the morning. She'll be there, too. I'm sorry to ask this, but I would really like it if you would go with me."

"Of course I'll be there. I love you too."

Maxwell stood up and embraced his wife with all his might, but nothing could console him. The idea of being a father scared him. But knowing Charmin would be there confirmed he had married the right woman. Charmin was sad to her core—she had wanted to be the one to give him a child, their child. Instead a complete stranger had given him the ultimate gift of a family, which made her heart ache.

"Well, it's a good thing we have a four-bedroom house," she said, laughing, trying to lighten the mood.

Maxwell didn't engage. Instead, he had a stern look of concern on his face. "I'll have to pay back child support and continued child support. I need to find Kevin's phone number. I need legal advice."

"How could you owe back support when you didn't know about the kids until today? She had a legal responsibility to tell you five years ago and instead chose not to. So I don't believe you will owe back support, only continued support with joint custody."

"That does make sense, but let me talk to Kevin to be sure we are covered."

"Okay, babe."

That evening, Maxwell fell into a deep sleep without wanting or needing sex. The scheduled appointment was for ten in the morning, and by seven, Maxwell was showered and dressed, talking on the phone downstairs.

"Sweetie, do you want breakfast?"

"No. I can't eat anything before the blood test."

"Okay."

Charmin finished dressing while Maxwell spoke to Kevin to understand his legal rights and options. At eight thirty, she walked downstairs to hear what Kevin had said.

"What did he say?"

"He'll meet us at the appointment because he wants to confirm everything and set up a meeting for joint custody."

"Okay."

The drive to the appointment was quiet and uncomfortable, more so for Maxwell than for Charmin. Instead, she couldn't wait to see Tanya again after her smug comment of "bye for now." Tanya had known why she'd come by—why had it taken her almost two weeks to confront Maxwell? What type of game was she playing? It couldn't be money—not driving an Acura TL. It had to be something else. Time would reveal her intent. Still, Charmin couldn't help but wonder at how her world had changed overnight—not necessarily for the worse, but they'd had a carefree life and out-of-the-box sex whenever the mood hit. No more late-night porn in the living room while eating popcorn and smoked peanuts and drinking Sam Adams. No more walking around the house nude or having sex on the kitchen table. Although Charmin was more conservative then Maxwell, she had learned to enjoy their lifestyle.

Maxwell parked the car at the clinic just before nine thirty and stared out the window as if contemplating something.

"Sweetie, are you okay?"

"Yes. I just can't believe what's happening to me."

"Honey, I'm here. We'll deal with this together. I forgot to ask—did she have the kids with her in the car?"

"No, she didn't. I think that is what's scaring me the most—actually meeting them after five years. I must seem like a total loser to them."

Maxwell started to sob again, and Charmin leaned toward him, resting her head against his shoulder until a knock against the window startled them both. It was Kevin.

"You guys okay?"

"Yeah, we're coming out. Give us a minute, okay?"

"Sure! We have time."

Maxwell exited the car first and extended his hands to Kevin. They chatted until Charmin joined them and they all walked into the clinic. Through the glass doors, Charmin noticed the same tall, attractive woman standing near two kids, who were sitting down. Tanya acknowledged them as they walked into the clinic.

"Hello." Tanya extended her hand to Charmin, and she reciprocated her greeting. Kevin headed toward the front desk to confirm their appointment, while Maxwell stared at the kids.

"Would you like to meet them, or do you want to wait for the blood test?" Tanya asked.

"Sure, I'll meet them. Why not?"

"Savannah and Miles, this is a special friend, Maxwell, and—I'm sorry, I don't know your name."

"Charmin."

"And this is his lovely wife, Charmin. Say hello, kids!"

"Hi."

"Hello."

Charmin noticed how well behaved and beautiful her kids were, although she didn't see any resemblance to Maxwell. Miles leaped off his chair and walked toward his mother, asking if he could go to the bathroom. Over hearing the conversation, Maxwell offered to take him since his nerves were getting the better of him. It was quite a sight for Charmin—Maxwell taking the hand of this little boy, possibly his son. Charmin felt confused, yet it was a precious moment that caused her to tear up a little.

"I'm really sorry to do this to you, but my kids are getting older and keep asking about their father. I realize after five years I have no right to intrude on your life this way, but I have a responsibility to my kids—plus Max has a right to know," Tanya stated.

"Why did you wait so long to tell him? What has changed?"

"Nothing, really. I'm pretty happy and can take care of my kids. They have a right to know their dad, and again, Max needed to know also. I really don't want anything from Max—just for him to be aware and decide what role, if any, he wants in their lives. I think that's fair."

"It is pretty fair. Thank you for being easy to work with and for giving us the opportunity to be a part of their lives. Better late than never, I always say."

"Yeah."

"Ms. Tanya Adams. Please approach the front desk," a nurse shouted.

"That's me!"

Tanya collected the kids and approached the desk, and the three were then whisked behind the door for the blood test. A few minutes later, Maxwell was also called. Charmin and Kevin were pacing around the waiting room for almost fifteen minutes before Tanya, the kids, and Maxwell came out.

"Well?" Charmin said.

"We have to wait for thirty minutes to get the results," Maxwell replied.

Those thirty minutes felt like forever. Finally, the nurse stepped out and handed Kevin an envelope.

"Okay, the moment of truth," Kevin said.

Maxwell seemed calm and unusually relaxed when Kevin confirmed they were his kids.

"Wow. Okay. I have kids. Thanks, Kevin, for being my legal advisor and friend. I'm a dad!"

"Congratulations, man. It will be okay. You and Charmin are good together and can handle anything."

"Thanks, man."

Charmin walked toward Tanya, smiling at her.

"I'm sure Kevin and Maxwell will be working out joint custody agreements with you, but could we take them out for ice cream or something to start to get to know them?"

"Sure. It will be good for both of you. I really enjoy being a mom. It will be okay. I know this is not what you had in mind, but things happen for a reason, and we were destined to be in your life. So I'd really like it if we could be friends. What do you say?"

"I'd like that too. Besides, we are family."

Maxwell walked toward Charmin, who was sitting on the chair near Savannah with Miles on her lap, laughing and playing with his little toy car. Maxwell embraced Tanya and exchanged words before taking a seat near Charmin to participate in the conversation with his kids.

"I've asked Tanya if we can take them out for ice cream or something. What do you think?" Charmin asked.

"That sounds good. Kevin will be scheduling a meeting with the county clerk so we can start the joint custody process."

Kevin walked toward Tanya and exchanged words before shaking her hand and saying good-bye to Maxwell and Charmin. They sat at the clinic for almost thirty minutes before heading out to Tanya's car so she could give them booster seats for the kids. She agreed to grant Maxwell until six that evening before she would pick them up. The kids seemed nervous when the booster seats were being exchanged and almost cried when Tanya got in her car after hugging them good-bye. Charmin and Maxwell embraced them as if they had known them forever. Together they filled the car with laughter and singing. Neither Savannah nor Miles shed a tear.

"Are you ready, Momma?" Maxwell said.

"I'm ready, Daddy-O."

They proceeded down the road en route to the mall, realizing they were now parents to the children sitting in the backseat. Charmin started singing the childhood melody "Row, Row, Row Your Boat." It seemed fitting.

Charmin